High Class

Mel Teshco

High Class

Dedication

To my patient husband who understands my love for writing is much MUCH stronger than my love for housework.

Dear Reader,

A huge thank you for reading about the VIP Desire women, where nothing is ever quite as it seems. These Agency women might earn huge money for their stunning good looks and skills in the bedroom, but they also carry plenty of secrets and emotional baggage ... enough to motivate them in choosing their profession.

I've loved uncovering Scarlet and Mackenzie's backstories, revealing their painful past and making their future seem uncertain at best. But one thing I *can* guarantee is their love for one another and the happily ever after they both deserve :)

Chapter One

Scarlet moved through the crowded room like she owned it. Tonight she wasn't barely noticeable Claire Davis. Tonight she was a paid seductress on the arm of one of the most famous men in the world.

She smoothed a manicured hand down her simple-but-exclusive white sheath dress, and checked her upswept hair remained in place. And all the while she smiled at the strangers her client, Amos Drynn, lead singer of Frankenstein's Blood, acknowledged with a vague nod of his head.

Many of those strangers were groupies and fans of Frankenstein's Blood. Many of those same fans were also the *crème de le crème* of the rich and elite, attending this latest good cause.

Tonight's charity auction was as much famed for its items up for bid as it was for its huge fundraising. Tonight Frankenstein's Blood were the main drawcard, and had on offer a one-hour performance for the highest bidder.

With all proceeds going to cancer research, it was a cause that touched her deeply. Her heart ached in an all too familiar way. It'd been a little over six years since her single mother had lost her fight against breast cancer, leaving behind three daughters, two of whom were twins and just barely in their teens.

"Don't look so serious," Amos teased, his muscled, tattooed arm pulling her close. "I don't pay you for that."

She pushed away the ache and arched a fine brow. "I'm also not paid to perform a blow job in front of three hundred people."

His lips curled into a grin, but before he had a chance to reply, a young woman with a pierced brow and nose ring brushed up against him. Her silver-studded thigh-high boots concealed more than her cut-off shorts and sparkly bikini top. "Here's my number," she crooned, pressing a slip of paper into his hands. "Call me anytime."

Amos declined, pushing past the woman of questionable age even as he muttered, "Unfortunately that young *lady* would do it for free."

Scarlet hid a grimace. She could fully understand why women came onto Amos. Even without his rock star status, he was gorgeous. But it didn't mean she'd join the queue in giving away her sexual expertise.

She had bills to pay, and sisters who relied on her—even more so now that they attended university.

Besides, the rock singer hired her *not* to service his carnal needs—he had any number of available groupies for that. Scarlet was little more than a professional front, a paid escort Amos wanted only to look pretty on his arm and to conduct half-decent social chitchat.

Unlike Mackenzie Smitherson. She shivered. That man had wanted more than a little from her. He'd taken her all. Again and again. And though he mightn't have tattoos and revealed only a business persona, she'd learned firsthand he didn't hold back in the bedroom.

He was as uninhibited as any wild rock star.

She turned to Amos, smiling at the singer's tough physique and big, inked, biceps. Strangely enough, she was comfortable with him, and liked the fact the bedroom didn't feature in their business transaction. Being with him was like hanging out with a big brother.

He paused, giving her a wink before he tucked a hand behind her head and pressed his lips to hers in a kiss that deliberately lingered.

Maybe not quite a big brother.

She leaned into him, going along with the charade that he was taken for the night. She held back a sigh. Although he was a great kisser, there was no spark, no magic in the act.

Not like she'd had with Mackenzie.

You have to stop thinking about that man!

She drew back, her face flushed. But not from the kiss ... far from it. Dwelling on Mackenzie and his bedroom skills was enough to send her knees weak and her pulse hammering. And that was despite the fact that after seven years in the sex industry she was becoming jaded.

"Are you okay?" Amos asked, his light blue eyes assessing.

She nodded. He paid her to put on an act, and that was what she'd do. "Never better."

Amos frowned. But before he could question her further, a paunchy, middle-aged man in a suit with a red bow tie approached him. He patted at his damp brow with a well-used handkerchief. "Sir, the auction is about to start."

Amos nodded and clasped her hand before they followed the older man into the hotel's auditorium. He leaned down and murmured, "Front row seats. Not too shabby."

He took a seat next to his equally famous band members, and she took the one next to him. She leaned her head against his shoulder and he drew an arm around her shoulders.

Her being with him mostly kept the groupies at bay, even as it added to his public persona. It was almost a given that a rock star had a different lover every week. A pity the media had already publicized them being together five times in the last six weeks. It meant their time together was coming to an end.

He'd probably hire another of the girls from the escort agency she worked for. Any one of her agency friends would be delighted by the easy money. Maybe she'd suggest Natalie. The blonde hadn't been herself since admitting to being in love with a married man who was seventeen years her senior. It would do Natalie good to spend some time with someone fun-loving and easygoing like Amos.

The bidding on a ten-day holiday on the Greek Islands commenced and Scarlet's introspection faded as she lost herself in the electric atmosphere. The holiday and each successive item sold for far more than their worth and she speculated whether people were bidding only to outdo one another and show off their wealth.

But it wasn't until the bidding started for the final item, the performance from Frankenstein's Blood, that her senses prickled. The hairs on the back of her neck lifted even before she turned and locked eyes with a man standing at the back of the room.

Mackenzie.

Her pulse fluttered as his dark, almost black eyes burned into hers. A potent mix of primal need and stark obsession. It was everything she felt for him and then some ... the same everything that had scared her away.

Her belly clenched. Her nipples tightened. Heat swept through her, no doubt flushing her pale-as-pale skin.

"Are you sure everything's okay?" Amos asked, his breath warm on her ear as he leaned close.

Mackenzie's eyes narrowed, a muscle jerking into life in his cheek before she tore her stare away and focused on Amos. "That's the second time you've had to ask me that." She managed a smile. "I'll have to give you a refund at this rate."

Amos grinned, leaning close to whisper, "Believe me, you're worth every cent. Groupies aren't my only concern."

So he'd had a girlfriend or mistress he no longer wanted around? She didn't ask; it was none of her business. She'd learned to listen to her clients, not ask questions. It was part of her service.

The bidding escalated quickly, every man and his dog seemingly wanting the band to play for them. Only when the figures had exceeded even the deepest pockets, and the bidding had died down, did she hear the all too familiar voice at the back of the room.

"Two million."

Amos lifted a bemused brow. "Wouldn't have picked that suited guy for a fan."

She couldn't even smile. Not this time. Few people saw past Mackenzie's business persona. Few people saw the pain he carried around inside him. A pain that seemed only to ease in the bedroom.

The gavel signified Mackenzie's win, and a hush fell over the room when Mackenzie nodded and strode forward to meet the band. At the front row his stare brushed over her before he introduced himself to the band members and shook their hands. "I believe you guys can play at any time, yes?"

Amos nodded. "That's right. We've cleared it with our label. We're free for the next two weeks."

Mackenzie nodded, satisfied. "Then you'll play for this audience, now."

Amos was taken aback. "Seriously?"

Mackenzie had always surprised her, but right then she was lost for words. Two million dollars for an impromptu performance? It was beyond excessive.

"It's for a good cause," he murmured, his gaze moving over her like a caress.

She swallowed hard, mesmerized by him, despite ... everything.

Then he turned back to Amos and the band members, and she could breathe again.

"I couldn't be more serious." Mackenzie paused a beat, and then asked, "You have your gear with you, yes?"

They nodded, and a bearded member of the group said, "We never leave home without it. Everything we need is stashed in my van."

Amos cocked an eyebrow. "Well then, boys. Guess we'd better get this show on the road."

She smiled at Amos when he looked at her, before she said, "Then I guess I'll wait for you here."

He nodded, and pushed through the crowd. She didn't turn to watch him leave. Not when every cell was attuned to Mackenzie. God, even had she wanted to run away, her trembling legs couldn't have supported her.

Not that she wanted to run. Far from it. She wanted to sit and drink in the man she'd been dreaming about for too long already. The man she'd pretended she didn't have feelings for, since the moment he'd taken more than a strictly business interest in her.

He'd recently had a haircut, the dark brown of his hair cropped close to his head. His cheekbones looked starker, almost angular, as though he'd lost his appetite. Then again, she supposed earning the big money came at a price. He worked hard and slept little.

He played even harder.

"Why are you doing this?" she asked.

His jaw hardened. "I need time alone with you. And if this is the only way I can get it, then so be it."

Her mouth dried. She shouldn't want this, but she did. She wanted it with everything she had.

"Scarlet," he finally acknowledged, her name sounding like a sexual promise and causing the whole world to fade around them, as though no-one else was near.

"Mack," she said softly, reverting to his nickname and unable to formulate even half a word more.

"You look stunning." His eyes flared. "Nothing's changed."

She dragged back her voice. "And I guess that's a compliment."

"One that I'm sure you receive every day from any number of men."

He hated that she was with other men. Yet another reason she couldn't see him anymore. She chewed her bottom lip. Her throat burned, along with the back of her eyes as all her repressed emotions threatened to burst free. "You know how I feel."

Liar. You might tell him you don't return his feelings, but how long will that hold up?

He sighed raggedly. “Yeah, I do.” He bent and cupped her chin, his thumb moving back and forth over her lips. “Doesn’t mean I have to accept it.”

Her belly did a slow flip-flop. “So … have you? Accepted it, I mean?”

He shook his head. “No, Scarlet, I haven’t. Though Lord only knows I’ve tried—too many times to count.”

The man in the red bow tie climbed onto the stage where the auction had been held. The moment he announced that Frankenstein’s Blood was going to play, noise erupted around them, cheers and excited chatter that barely infiltrated Scarlet’s mind.

She was too busy staring at Mackenzie. In that moment, all her social graces had been left behind. She should stand too, anything to try and wrest back some kind of advantage.

But then his thumb moved to trace over her bottom lip. He bent his head, his voice in her ear sending goose bumps down her spine. “It nearly killed me to see another man kiss you.”

She closed her eyes. Little wonder Mackenzie had been front and center in her head tonight. She’d been attuned to him because he’d been in the same room, watching her with Amos. She forced her eyes back open. “It nearly killed me knowing you were with Brandy,” she admitted huskily.

His eyes darkened. “You didn’t want me.”

Her chest ached. *I did … oh, how I did. But I had to protect myself.*

His stare softened. “Brandy’s beautiful. But she’s not you. Not even close. No woman holds a candle next to you.”

Scarlet smiled. Brandy—Kate—was still beautiful even after having twin boys a month earlier. Kate no longer worked at the agency, and Scarlet couldn’t be happier for her. Kate truly deserved her devoted husband and happily-ever-after.

But no one was irreplaceable. With Kate now gone, Scarlet, along with Tiffany and Savannah, had taken the gorgeous new call girl,

Anna—who'd adopted the working name of Candy—under their wing. Inviting her to their lunches and shopping outings, and giving advice whenever she needed some. Anna, with all her innocence ... Scarlet wasn't looking forward to the day she saw the young woman's eyes harden.

The band set up their equipment and began a prerequisite warm up, plucking guitar strings and running through a sound check. She pulled free from Mackenzie's clasp and dragged her eyes away to focus on Amos.

She'd thrown out the rule book tonight. Amos was her client and she was all but rejecting him. She couldn't afford to piss him off and risk ruining her call girl reputation. Not if she wanted to continue supporting her twin sisters, Danni and Tina.

With their mother dead and buried, and their father a distant memory, it'd fallen on her shoulders to keep her sisters clothed, fed and educated. A twinge of resentment flared, and then died away. She'd do anything for the twins. Anything to make sure they had careers they loved, careers that weren't in the sex industry. Careers that were safe and even a little bit predictable.

Mackenzie's eyes narrowed. But whatever he was about to say died in the ruckus immediately after Amos introduced himself and the crowd surged forward.

Scarlet stood, her attention staying on Mackenzie as she shouted above the noise, "I can never be what you want."

As the band broke into sound, she pushed past Mackenzie and headed toward the exit.

"Scarlet, wait!"

She made it to just outside the auditorium before Mackenzie caught her arm and spun her around. His eyes blazed. "I'm not letting you go. Not this time."

She stared up at him, her emotions bubbling over. "I'm not sure I even want you to," she admitted. "Not tonight."

He kissed her then, with more desperate hunger and skill than she could bear. She barely noticed him lifting her against his chest and carrying her away from the noise. She was lost in the kiss, reveling in sensation.

Even guilt over leaving Amos faded away, just the same as Amos's honeyed, baritone voice did when Mackenzie stepped into a room and kicked shut its door. The quiet seemed almost as loud when he turned her around and pressed her back against a wall, his big male body surrounding hers.

She was glad of the shadowy room, where light from the corridor outside was the only illumination to chase away complete darkness. She didn't want him to read her face. Didn't want him to know exactly how much she wanted him.

She was already wet for him, her body a willing recipient to whatever he desired. One touch and she was his. One kiss and she was lost. Lord help her, one last time in his arms, and then she'd walk away from him for good.

He slid his zipper down with a rasp before he undid a button, his pants then dropping low, followed by his underwear. He didn't bother to step out of them. There was too much urgency, too much heat.

With quick, economical movements, he unwrapped a foil from his pocket, and rolled the condom onto his straining shaft. Her heart rate bucked when he lifted her dress and slid aside her lacy thong, then one-handed his cock to center it at her core.

She was hazily aware this sexual encounter was wrong on too many levels, but she didn't much care. She wanted this. *Needed* this.

His eyes glinted above hers about the same time he drove forward, burying himself deep inside her. Her breath hissed sharply at the pleasure–pain. He'd always been big, always stretched her to the limit. Yet her body readily accepted his impressive length and breadth, readily accepted any of his sexual demands.

She didn't need to pretend sex with this man was wonderful. Not when being with him felt all kinds of right. Not when her every nerve ending burned in his presence, and then exploded the moment they joined.

With his deliberately slow pumps in and out, she was already heading toward the place only Mackenzie knew how to take her. Then he abruptly pulled out, spun her around and leaned her against a huge table. A staff room table, she realized hazily.

His knee between her legs caused her to part them. Then he leaned over her and guided his cock once more between the petals of her labia. "Does your client make you feel this good?" he asked harshly.

She gasped as he entered her then in one long stroke, a hand bunching in her hair and bringing her head back.

"Does he know how you love being taken from behind? How you love your hair pulled just like this?"

"No." Her voice cracked, and she felt his smirk, before his mouth latched onto the side of her neck and his strokes in and out increased until nothing could stop the freight train of an orgasm from ripping through her and tossing her high.

Mackenzie let out a guttural moan as her inner muscles clamped him tight, and he too came, her scalp burning as his hand tightened momentarily, before releasing her.

She was still sucking in breaths from her dizzying ride when he pulled free, disposed of the condom, and then turned her around to face him.

"This isn't the end between us, Scarlet," he murmured huskily. His expression might be shadowed, but she sensed his intensity. "It's just the beginning."

Chapter Two

Scarlet refastened her hair into its usual topknot as she walked back to the auditorium with Mackenzie by her side, his vanilla-and-spice cologne clinging to her skin. Her body hummed with sexual release, even as her emotions were tightly coiled.

They didn't talk; words weren't necessary after the intimacy they'd shared minutes earlier. They didn't need speech to know there was a bond now between them, something that had shifted the boundaries.

It scared her more than ever.

The music pulsated, loud and seductive in the auditorium, with Amos crooning out a rock ballad that had his audience mesmerized.

Mackenzie placed a hand on her lower back to guide her past scattered groups of people who danced and swayed, and she shivered at his possessive touch. She might be jaded with other men, but with Mackenzie, every look and touch was exciting.

She took the seat she'd abandoned earlier, while Mackenzie took Amos's seat, his arm curling around her shoulders and leaving no one in doubt just who she was with now.

He leaned close, so that she could hear him above the music. "Amos isn't half bad," he conceded.

She nodded, and he turned his ear to her mouth so she could answer without shouting. "He's a celebrated music artist for a reason."

He twisted to face her, a hand cupping her chin before he leaned forward. "You won't be fucking him tonight."

She glared. He didn't need to know she wouldn't be doing that with Amos anyway. That was *her* business, not his. "Amos is my client."

"So replace him with me."

She arched a brow. "And my other clients?"

He leaned closer. "You don't need them. You only need me."

Yearning filled her, even as she pushed the emotion away and refuted, "Hardly a long term solution."

His dark eyes held hers, conveying his desire. His need. His obsession. "We'll start short term. A weekend together. Then worry about long term later."

She blew out a slow breath and shook her head. "My agency doesn't do exclusive."

It was his turn to cock a brow. "I paid two million for fifteen minutes of your time. Imagine what I'd be willing to pay your agency for a weekend."

She bit her bottom lip, torn between excitement and fear at his proposition. She stood, all but shouting to make herself heard. "Talk to Maisey." The woman not only had a mane of tawny hair like a lion's, she ran the agency as though her workers were her pride. "If she agrees, then ... you have me for the weekend."

She ignored a sharp stab of despair, knowing that would never happen. Maisey wouldn't agree to Mackenzie's proposition. Maisey always did what was best for the agency, because in the escort business, reputation was everything.

He stood too. "Oh, she'll agree." He slid a glance at the singer on stage, whose tight leather pants and tousled, blond–brown hair left the ladies swooning. "Just ... don't be with that man tonight. Don't be with *any* man."

His demand was beyond arrogant, even ludicrous for someone of her profession. But she found herself nodding anyway, told herself it was because she could safely make that promise when she was with Amos. "Fine."

He inclined his head, then reached out a hand and brushed his thumb beneath her jaw. Turning on his heel, he left the auditorium.

Left the band not even halfway through the performance he'd paid a small fortune to hear.

Left her with yet another little piece of her heart going right along with him.

Mackenzie took the hotel's private elevator to the top floor of his penthouse suite. Striding through the expansive living space, he opened the sliding glass door and stepped outside onto the balcony.

He needed some air. If only that same air wasn't saturated with the incredible music from Frankenstein's Blood, who still played eighteen floors below. He didn't want to think about the lead singer being with Scarlet, didn't want to imagine them in bed together.

If only his mind didn't conjure up a naked Scarlet, her beautiful tits bouncing rhythmically, her upswept hair dragged free and framing her gorgeous face and body as she fucked the rock idol who possibly half the women on the planet lusted after.

His chest burned, his jaw aching with tension as he squeezed his eyes closed and dragged a hand over his face.

Though Mackenzie had never had trouble attracting the opposite sex, he knew whatever insecurities he might harbor were now exposed, a nerve deep inside that was damaged and raw. Revealing the boy who'd watched his father beat up his mother. The same boy knocked to the ground for trying to protect her.

A boy who'd been powerless and defenseless.

His hands curled around the balcony railing. He wasn't that boy anymore. He'd grown up, burning with ambition and starving for control. Now he was one of Australia's richest and most powerful men. People respected him, took notice of him.

Scarlet, on the other hand ...

He barely noticed the twinkling lights of Sydney Harbour, the ferries and boats churning past. His hands tightened as he replayed the exquisite act of taking Scarlet in the hotel's staff room. She'd been dynamite in his arms, responsive to his every touch, her body attuned to his in a way no other woman had ever been before.

God help him, even the smattering of freckles on her chest turned him on. He loved to lick her silky soft skin, before moving to her creamy, rose-tipped tits and suckling them until she arched against him with a gasp ...

Get a grip, man. She's trained to make you believe you're the only man she wants.

His belly hardened as his mind flashed to the kiss Scarlet had shared with Amos. He sucked in a deep breath, forcing back control. He'd been ready to tear the couple apart so he could smash a fist into Amos's face. Been prepared to do whatever it took to make sure the singer never kissed or touched Scarlet again.

Hypocrite.

He hadn't exactly been celibate in the eighteen months since Scarlet had tossed him aside, as though his money and status meant nothing. He'd foolishly believed fucking his way through a dozen beautiful mistresses and call girls would help him to forget her.

Scarlet, with her intelligent green eyes, slender, toned body and gorgeous flame-red hair was nothing like the blonde, voluptuous women he'd once dated. Yet she filled his mind to breaking point. Perhaps it was the soul-deep recognition of vulnerability and strength that he also carried around inside himself. An attraction that couldn't be denied no matter how much they tried.

His denial had finally been nipped in the bud when his last three sexual encounters had been with beautiful red-headed women. All of whom had made him feel nothing except an even deeper longing for Scarlet.

It was why he'd gone to great lengths to ensure tonight's charity auction would be held at one of his hotels. Had taken even greater care to ensure he'd meet Scarlet tonight, even if that meant seeing her with the client who was the charity event's main drawcard.

But would Scarlet be turned on or off knowing just how very far he was prepared to go to make her his own?

He pushed away from the rails. Pivoting on his heel, he headed to his fully stocked bar. He needed a drink, something double strength to ease the ache within. Then he'd make a phone call to the VIP Desire Agency and ensure Scarlet was his for the weekend.

He poured himself a good splash of whiskey and drank down the burning liquid, before he exhaled heavily. Yes, he'd make that phone call. And then he'd catch one last glimpse of Scarlet before he retired for the night and figured out how the hell he'd make theirs a permanent relationship.

Scarlet returned to her seat when Amos finished his hour-long performance and finally pushed his way through the admiring crowd.

He sat near her, deliberately facing away from anyone who might try and steal more of his time. "I hate to say it, but that man who bid on us definitely wasn't a fan of mine."

Heat flared up her neck. She delicately cleared her throat. "Why do you say that?"

He smiled. "He looked like a man who'd found his wife cheating on him. Is he a client of yours?"

She nodded. "Yes. Or at least, he used to be."

Amos chuckled. "I'm thinking he will be again very soon, yes?"

She swallowed back denial. Amos might be paying her to be with him, but he didn't pay her to lie. Not to mention he was a wonderful man, deserving of the truth. "Only if he finds a way to get past Maisey's shrewd business sense."

His smile faded as he searched her face. He seemed concerned for her well-being. "He looks like a man who gets what he wants. And he definitely wanted you." He lifted a hand to curl a piece of her hair behind an ear. "Guess he'll be happy to know our time was coming to an end anyway."

She pushed away a raft of sadness. No client lasted forever. She'd do well to remember it. "Yes, I guess he will." She blinked. "If you're interested, I know someone in the agency who'd be perfect for you."

❧

Claire—she used the name Scarlet only when she was an escort—did some quick stretches, before she crouched and laced up her sneakers. Heading out the front door of her small three-bedroom home, she broke into a run.

She always enjoyed her early morning exercise. Staying active was as big a part of her routine as sleeping and eating. In her line of business she had to stay fit, had to be in shape for those men who enjoyed lying back while she did all the work.

She grinned. Paying outrageous sums of money gave her clients that privilege and then some. Unlike Mackenzie, who got off on giving her pleasure first. He was the only client who made her climax for real. She shivered. He was also the only man who gave her goose bumps just by thinking about him.

She turned left at a little quaint cottage with an overgrown garden. Mrs. Gracie was an elderly neighbor she often visited, a woman who'd known her mother, and who'd seen Claire and her sisters grow up. The same woman who'd raised her grandson, Bradley—one of Claire's best friends—before he'd left to backpack around the world.

But Mrs. Gracie was getting old and frail now, and her garden was obviously too hard to maintain. Claire made a mental note to visit her again soon, and give her a helping hand.

She crossed the road to the next block, where Sydney suburban homes were giving way to chic apartments. On her income, she could afford something quite a bit nicer than the small, one-bathroom, red-brick home that was faded with age. But when that same home her mother had once rented had come up for sale three years earlier, Claire couldn't give it up.

There'd been too many happy memories, too many birthdays and Christmases. Too much of her mother still lingering in the home to simply walk away from it all. It was also the home her sisters had grown up in, making it their one stability in life. Lord only knew Danni and Tina needed all the stability they could get.

Besides, the money she'd saved by not living a flashy lifestyle went into providing for her sisters' futures. She hadn't become an escort to live at the best address or eat the finest food. She enjoyed home-cooked meals made on her old electric stove as much as she did the latest and greatest cuisine she sampled all too often with her clients.

Mackenzie loved simple fare too. He'd often taken her to a local pub for dinner, where they'd enjoyed steak, chips and salad, or a good old-fashioned chicken schnitzel. She learned a lot about her clients from the places they went and the food and drinks they consumed.

She'd guarantee Mackenzie's upbringing had been far simpler than the life he presently led.

She rounded a corner, nodding at a young woman who was speed-walking with a stroller from the other direction.

Claire slowed and pressed a hand to her belly, pushing away a sudden maternal urge. She *didn't* want children. Bringing up hormonal teen girls had surely been enough.

Except an image of a little boy with Mackenzie's sharp cheekbones and flashing, brilliant dark eyes, and a little girl with Mackenzie's dark brown hair and long lashes, couldn't be suppressed.

She grimaced. No. She wouldn't even think about babies. Besides the fact it was undesirable in her line of work to have a baby, she'd never put herself in that position. Never give a man the ability to walk away from her or her child.

She'd learned that the hard way after watching her father walk away from his family.

Better to be single and independent. Better to never rely on anyone but herself.

She surged forward, pushing her legs hard. Pushing herself to *not* think about anything but deep, steady breaths as she ran.

She succeeded ... to a point. Until she became aware of a gold-colored, late model sedan following her. Her pulse quickened, a knot of anxiety forming in her belly. The classy car screamed money, like something one of her clients would drive. She turned another corner and the car slowly followed.

Her throat dried. Had a client somehow learned her address? Or had someone nearby discovered what she did for a living? She'd done her utmost to conceal her profession and keep away potential crazies. Perhaps she hadn't done enough.

She'd had a couple of clients in the past who'd been forceful and even a little hostile. The agency had firmly shown their asses out the door ... but not before those same men had used her body to their satisfaction.

She locked those memories away into the back of her mind where they belonged. It was the biggest drawback to her profession, and yet another reason she never wanted her sisters to consider the option of sleeping with men for money. Once Danni and Tina had finished university and entered their chosen profession, she intended to leave the VIP Desire Agency, maybe even take up some kind of study herself.

The gold car pulled in front of her and drew to a stop at the curb. Her breath caught, and as she turned to run across the road, away from even a hint of danger, Mackenzie climbed from the back of the sedan.

His white teeth glinted and his eyes ran approvingly over the black tights and pink crop top she reserved for running and the gym.

She stilled, blinking at him even as relief was superseded by outrage. "You!"

He arched a dark brow. "Did you think I might have been someone else?" His expression mightn't betray him, but his tone revealed his censure.

"I had *no* idea who was following me," she snapped, her heart rate not settling even a little at seeing him. "*No*-one knows where I live."

He shrugged. "It was easy enough to follow you home last night."

"Seriously?" Her insides roiled at his arrogance. Had he wanted her address, or to see if she'd break her word and sleep with Amos? She stepped jerkily toward him. "You've gone too far."

"Not far enough, Scarlet."

She shook her head, remembering she was no longer Claire, the everyday girl next door. She was Scarlet, the escort. "You're not even a client."

"But I am." At her hiss of disbelief, he added, "I've managed to book you for all this weekend. Friday night until Sunday night."

She stared. Never in a million years had she thought he'd get past Maisey's bulldog defences. She should have known better. And that was despite the fact she'd already been booked solid for at least a month in advance—all the VIP Desire Agency girls were. The agency was an exclusive establishment, where even the wealthiest clients had to gain approval before they were put on a waiting list.

She crossed her arms. "Where? And how much?"

"At my holiday house in the Blue Mountains." He stepped forward, closing the gap between them before he trailed a hand along her jaw. "As for how much ... do you always value your self-worth by the figures you earn?"

She jerked her head away. "I don't do what I do for charity. Not everyone can afford to pay two million dollars for fifteen minutes of my time."

He nodded. "True." His dark eyes gleamed, but he didn't touch her this time when he ended the conversation with, "Expect a phone call from Maisey. I'll see you tonight at six. Pack casual and warm."

He didn't give her the figure he'd been willing to pay Maisey to scratch off two of her most prominent clients for the weekend.

Chapter Three

Late afternoon sunlight streamed through Claire's bedroom window as she zipped up her suitcase and took a final, long look around her house. Dust motes danced gently in the sunbeam, the hallway clock ticking loudly.

It felt so empty. With her sisters now boarding at university, the house all but rang out with hollowness. She'd often wondered if she could survive the twins' hormonal years, but surely living with that was better than living with this ... nothingness.

She exhaled softly. She might spend half of her time with men, but she'd never felt more lonely. Never before had she wished for the seemingly harassed, frenetic lifestyle she'd witnessed so many young mothers and wives live.

Her cell phone rang, startling her. Caller ID revealed it was Maisey, doing her mandatory, pre-check call. Once Maisey was satisfied everything was on track for the weekend ahead, Scarlet disconnected. Then with a final look around the too-quiet house, she stepped outside in black skinny jeans, high-heeled leather boots and a cream and grey-flecked knit jumper to wait for the agency's town car.

Maisey had made arrangements with Mackenzie on where to meet. No client was allowed to know where she lived. No client knew where *any* of the escorts lived, period. Their privacy was to be protected at all costs, because without it, their safety was put at a much higher risk.

Despite Mackenzie's wealth, if Maisey discovered he'd learned her address, she had no doubt he wouldn't be welcomed back as a VIP client.

If you really want him out of your life, then you'll tell Maisey the truth.

She pushed away the snide little voice, and then nodded at the driver as he tucked her suitcase into the trunk, and she climbed into the back seat. Fifteen minutes later, the town car pulled up at a service station, where a big black SUV waited.

Mackenzie was out of the SUV and had her back door open almost before the sedan had stopped. Faded, snug-fitting jeans caressed his thighs and buttocks, and lovingly defined the bulge of his cock. She tore her eyes away, focusing on his crisp white T-shirt and dark-colored jacket. She blinked. Damn, he wore his clothes well. She looked higher. His warm eyes brushed over her, his features not quite so stark. Almost as though he'd relaxed at seeing her arrival.

He cradled her forearm as he helped her alight, confirming her thoughts when he murmured, "Thank you for coming."

Her chin lifted and her hand tightened on her clutch bag. "It's my job."

His eyes narrowed and his jaw tensed. But she didn't find relief at knowing she'd scored a point against him. Far from it.

"Indeed," he said quietly, even as he took hold of her suitcase and escorted her toward his SUV.

It wasn't until he drove out of the city and onto a remote stretch of highway, where darkness fell all around them and lightning flickered behind distant clouds, that she turned to him and said, "I'm sorry."

He turned to her. "What for?"

"For trying to bring you down to my level."

He turned his focus back to the road, but she knew his attention was all on her. "And what level would that be?" he asked softly.

"The level of doubts and insecurities I seem to have whenever I'm around you."

Passing headlights gave her a glimpse of his forbidding face, another flash soon after revealing a slightly less stern profile. He sighed, as though expelling any lingering tautness. "You're scared of what we could have."

"What we could have?" she echoed, her heart thumping and her throat going dry.

He turned to her then, another set of incoming headlights showing his intense stare. "Yes. We're attracted to one another more than just physically. And you know as well as I do that it needs to be further explored."

She blinked. "We share a business transaction. Nothing more."

"Really?" His stare had turned back to the road, but the strength of his emotions rolled off him in waves. "What if after this weekend you're proven wrong?"

She couldn't stop yearning from cramping in her belly. "I'll worry about that *if* it ever happens."

Not when, please God, not when.

She'd tried to walk away from Mackenzie once to save her heart, she didn't know if she was capable of doing it twice. She'd seen her mother go through hell because she'd fallen in love with a faithless man, and she refused to follow in her mother's footsteps.

But had she already left it too late?

She didn't have an answer to that. What could she say about the very thing that scared her the most?

The wind picked up as they began the ascent toward the Blue Mountains, leaves and twigs swirling across the road and treetops swaying. She peered out the window, watching lightning blaze across the sky. It looked like one hell of a storm, and they were heading directly into it.

Mackenzie didn't seem concerned; he drove the car effortlessly, his control at the wheel seemingly as confident as it was behind the helm of his global empire. It was common knowledge that he owned a chain of luxury five-star hotels, liquor stores and restaurants right across the globe, making him one of Australia's most wealthy and successful men.

As his paid escort, she wasn't expected to ask about his personal life, not unless he wanted to spill his secrets of his own accord. Even so, she recognized he was as emotionally scarred as he was materially healthy. That he carried his wounds all on the inside drew her to him all the more. Despite his worldly success, he was a warrior fighting his own personal demons.

He indicated a couple of times, turning off the main road and onto a much narrower sealed road. A few minutes later he pulled onto yet another road and negotiated a winding track that climbed steeply before the road abruptly levelled out and the headlights glinted on a log cabin's windows.

The scent of incoming rain announced its arrival just seconds before the heavens unleashed a torrential downpour. Winds even stronger than before lashed at the car and buckled even the biggest of trees. Mackenzie parked beside the cabin and flicked off the headlights, before he drew off his jacket and said wryly, "Looks like we'll be getting a little wet."

She nodded, strangely invigorated by the storm. "It looks like it."

He climbed out of his seat and ran around to her side of the car, the rain drumming on the car's roof and the wind howling. Helping her out, he held his jacket over their heads while they ran to the front door.

Scarlet laughed giddily at the total wildness of it all. Her life was dictated by rules. It was energizing to have those rules tossed away with the winds and enjoy the spontaneity.

Despite Mackenzie's jacket, they were both drenched through long before he pushed an old-fashioned key into the lock and thrust the door open. Even with his arm around her, she all but fell inside. He released her and slammed the door shut. But the barely audible click of the light switch didn't yield any light.

Pitch blackness surrounded them, and Scarlet's breath caught in her throat, her humor fading as the dark and dank cold quickly set in.

"The wind must have knocked out a power line," he muttered.

She pushed up the sodden sleeves of her jumper and rubbed at her bare, goose bumped arms. "Then I guess we'll have to keep each other warm."

She sensed his approach even before his hands landed on her shoulders, his silhouette shadowy and barely visible. "You're freezing." He took hold of the hem of her jumper, and her arms went into the air obediently before he dragged the sodden jumper along with her tee up and over her head.

The clothes thudded heavily to the floor, and her nipples strained against the thin material of her bra. But her pebbled nipples weren't just from the cold. Although it was dark, she felt his eyes devouring her, as though he could easily see her partial nakedness. She had no doubt his brilliant memory filled in any blanks.

She swallowed hard. This once she was unsure of what to do. All her escort experience and business sense yielded to the churning emotions and needs filling her to the brim.

Mackenzie too seemed swept up in that same whirlpool of yearning when he said her name in a low, hoarse tone like a benediction. Then he cupped the back of her head, his mouth moving over hers in a kiss that made her forget about the cold, made her forget about everything but his male heat and hardness.

The noise of the rain and the wind and the night's blackness cocooned them, until all she knew was Mackenzie and his mouth, his hands moving up and down her hips, his cock bulging against her belly in his wet jeans. His kiss deepened, his velvet tongue pushing into her mouth, exploring and stroking. Until she was moaning against his lips and he was drinking in the sound.

He drew back, his dark, sensual voice underscored with a thread of concern. "Get undressed. I'll find you a towel."

She did as he asked, the heavy rain and wind drowning out his retreating footsteps. She hugged herself, but it was her emotions that made her feel vulnerable and exposed, not the fact she was naked.

Being with Mackenzie was dangerous on too many levels. No matter how much she resisted he dug past her defenses, leaving the walls around her heart weaker with each invasion. Somehow she had to remember this was her job, nothing more. That Mackenzie was her client, not someone capable of breaking her.

Thunder rumbled outside, masking any noise. But she sensed Mackenzie's return like he was a part of her.

He didn't say anything, just gently dragged the towel back and forth across her shoulders, along her spine and buttocks and then the backs of her legs. When he proceeded to do the same at her front, she closed her eyes and leaned a little closer, her breath hitching and her legs going weak.

For a man with such big hands, he'd always had a deft touch. Always been the only man who'd ever brought her to ecstasy. He bent and placed the towel between her thighs then slowly see-sawed the towel forward and back, scraping the soft material across her clit until she was breathless and moaning.

Lightning crackled outside, illuminating the room and revealing Mackenzie's intensity. As though pleasing her was his one ambition. As though gaining her submission was his greatest win.

What scared her most was that he didn't even need to try. He was a master craftsman and she was putty in his too-capable hands.

But just when orgasm was seconds away from rippling through her body in much needed release, Mackenzie straightened and drew the towel up and around her. "We'll continue this ... after I light the fire and get you warm."

Her breath stuttered in rhythm to her pulse. She wanted him to finish what he'd started *now.* Not in half an hour. "Bastard," she whimpered.

He bent his head close to hers and his chuckle sent goose bumps down her spine. But it wasn't until he sucked her lobe into his mouth that her inner barometer charged straight past the *fuck me immediately* level.

"Call me what you want," he murmured throatily, "because I plan on making you ten times hotter before you come and come … and come."

Her pussy clenched, and the moisture pooling at her core had nothing to do with the rain. "You're paying me to make *you* come," she croaked.

His fingertips grazed under her jaw. "I do that every night just thinking about you, and what we share in the bedroom." His chuckle sounded deeper, darker. "But right now, tasting your cum on my lips and tongue, and seeing your juices glaze my fingers and dick is everything I want and need."

She swallowed hard, before he stepped back and added, "I'd better light that fire before my dick takes over my brain."

She stood silent and shaking with lust as intermittent lightning showed him stacking kindling and bigger hunks of wood over scrunched-up newspaper. A match flared and he set the tiny flame onto the paper before it lit and quickly caught hold.

She blew out a soft breath, glancing at the gloomy interior. The growing fire caused shadows to flicker and dance across the log walls of the dining and lounge area. The room was stark, with no pictures or mementos that she could see. Nothing that was personal at all.

She frowned. She'd never been inside his home, had no idea where he even lived. He'd always taken her to fancy hotels and apartments for the night. His holiday home was as close as she'd come to his private living space. But with no photos or knickknacks, she had no further clues to his life.

Did his intense privacy indicate issues with trust?

Aside from the front and back entrance, there were only two other doors leading to rooms. She guessed one opened into a bathroom and toilet, the other to a single bedroom—and no doubt to a king-size bed where Mackenzie would make love to her most of the weekend.

She shivered with longing. *Don't ever forget you work in the sex industry. You fuck men like Mackenzie, not make love.*

He stood then and turned around, his eyes glinting with the flare of the fire in the background. "Come here," he said huskily.

She smiled, and let go of the towel to reveal all her splendour. His eyes burned hotter than the fire when she sashayed toward him, undoing her hair and allowing it to fall in a ripple of movement almost to her waist.

No matter her true feelings for him, she'd never forget she was first and foremost a call girl, paid to get him off.

His jaw tightened with lust. "You're fucking gorgeous."

"And you're handsome as hell," she retorted, winding her arms behind his nape and standing on tiptoe to kiss his sexy mouth.

He kissed her back like he owned her, the scrape of his stubble only adding to the intensity of the moment. He even tasted amazing, mint and spice, his lips lush but firm. She slid her palms down his arms and tucked her hands beneath his tee, stroking over his wet, but warm skin, where his tight core muscles rippled with every little movement.

Though he wasn't bulked up like a thickset bodybuilder, his corded strength never ceased to amaze her. He could probably bench press two of her without any great effort. He made her feel safe and secure, like he could protect her against anything.

The woman who stole his heart would be very lucky indeed.

She shoved aside the green-eyed monster and instead lost herself to his skilled lips and mouth. They didn't stop kissing until he pulled back to strip off his shirt, then his jeans and boxer briefs. Her eyes widened in familiar appreciation at his body. Sheer perfection. His every dip and plane might be imprinted on her brain, but she doubted she'd ever stop ogling him.

He tugged her back towards him, his mouth connecting to hers once again and his cock pressing thick and insistent against her belly. "You don't know how much I need this ... need you," he said against her mouth, his voice hoarse.

"The feeling's mutual," she breathed. But he wasn't to know she was speaking the truth. He wasn't to know she wasn't being Scarlet, paid call girl. She was being Claire, homemaker and everyday girl next door.

He tilted her back, and laid her down beside the fireplace. A soft, thick rug pressed beneath her spine as he moved over her, his eyes glinting from the reflection of the fire. Scarlet blinked up at him. The storm might still be raging outside, but passion raged just as ferociously between them.

Her breasts scraped across his chest, arousing nerve endings in her nipples, and causing her pussy to spasm with need.

Placing most of his weight on a forearm, Mackenzie slid a hand between her thighs and parted the petals of her sex, a finger sliding deep inside her wet heat. When he took up a rhythm and bent his head to suckle her breast, she arched with a gasp.

Holy shit. How did he so effortlessly generate such heat and pleasure? She'd been with many talented men in the bedroom, and yet not one of them had come close to making her feel this good.

A pity that just as she reached for the peak, he paused, and waited for her to cool off before he started the foreplay all over again.

"Don't do this to me," she whimpered, firelight flickering his profile in and out of shadow and making him look like some barbarian of old.

"You want me to stop?"

She shook her head, but he withdrew anyway, only to stroke the flesh around her clit, being careful not to touch her quivering mass of nerves.

"Is this what you want?" he asked.

"Yes ... *no*. I don't know!" she gasped.

A quirk touched his lips, before he crawled down her body and said, "Perhaps this?"

Parting her labia, he lowered his head to her mound. When his mouth latched onto her clit and he suckled, she shrieked at the high voltage electricity sparking into life, his tongue flicking and licking. She lasted perhaps ten or twenty seconds before she exploded with one orgasm, and then another, while Mackenzie tasted her essence, lapping at her like she was the finest cuisine.

Giving her one last, long lick, he looked up at her with glinting eyes. "Better now, baby?"

"Yes." *Hell, yes.*

He kneeled between her legs, and pushed her knees back so that she was exposed to him. "I plan on making it even better for you."

She was too drowsily sated to even think of a response, let alone put a stop to his next round of seduction. But by the time her hazy mind processed him centering his cock at her core, before he thrust forward and filled her to the hilt, it was much too late.

She gasped, equally stimulated by his delicious entry and horrified by his uncovered cock. "You didn't use protection!"

He looked down at her. His stare fairly glowed, revealing no regrets. "You're on the pill, and I know you use condoms when you're with your clients, just as I always do." He leaned forward and brushed a strand of hair back from her face. "Baby, our first time without condoms should be with one another."

She stared up at him, too turned on to be mad, though there was a simmer of reproach deep in her belly that would boil over at some point. "You should have asked first."

He nodded, before bending further and kissing her with a slow tenderness that caused her heart to melt. Until he pulled back and murmured, "After this weekend, I hope I'll never need to ask again."

If Scarlet had even one iota of sense she'd put him in his place right there and then. But the moment he moved his hips and stroked long and deep inside her, she was lost to everything but sensation.

Lost to the one man she'd desperately tried to forget and stay away from.

She hadn't tried hard enough.

Then he was leaning forward and kissing her again, taking ownership of her mouth like he already had with the rest of her body, sucking in her cries of stark passion while stroking long and deep inside her. Stroking faster and harder until she couldn't hold back on the climax that overtook her, body and soul.

Couldn't stop her mewl of delight as she skyrocketed to the heavens and back.

When his seed shot warm and deep inside her, and the walls echoed with her name being shouted long and loud, she couldn't stop her heart from melting for him all the more.

He withdrew from her and pulled her into his arms, the fire crackling and hissing behind them while the rain and thunder continued unabated. She squeezed her eyes closed. Had she ever felt happier, yet more confused and adrift?

Chapter Four

Scarlet woke to the aromatic scent of coffee and the pre-dawn sounds of a dozen different birdcalls. No rain drummed on the roof and no wind lashed at the windows. She reached out. And no hot male body was stretched out beside her.

Her eyes flicked open as Mackenzie strode over in nothing but low-slung jeans, his skin lightly tanned and his face in shadow. He crouched beside her with a mug of steaming coffee. Hot coals in the fireplace gleamed behind him, throwing his face into sharp relief and pushing back the shadows of the still-dark room.

She blinked and asked sleepily, "The power's not back on?"

He shook his head. "No, I made use of the gas stove."

She sat and accepted the mug, not missing the gleam of appreciation in his eyes as he took in her nakedness that caused her nipples to bead. She pushed away self-consciousness. As an escort such an emotion shouldn't even be an afterthought.

It was enough that she had to drag her own stare away from the six-pack of his belly, his corded arms and shoulders. Not to mention the light dusting of hair that trailed temptingly past the waistband of his denim.

She took a sip of the hot brew and stretched a little, withholding a wince. She'd slept like a baby in Mackenzie's arms, but though the rug had been soft enough, it wasn't the quality inner spring mattress she was accustomed to sleeping on.

Mackenzie straightened, and pulled on a dark T-shirt and jacket he'd slung on the dining chair nearby. "Time to get up and dressed," he murmured huskily, gesturing to her suitcase he'd placed near the front door. "There's something I want to show you."

Not even ten minutes later she was dressed in jeans and a canary yellow, long-sleeved shirt, and had her hair drawn back into a topknot. She felt almost human again after drinking her coffee, and as she followed Mackenzie outside to a crystal-clear, star-studded sky that showed the vaguest hint of dawn in the air, any lingering tiredness fell away.

The fresh, clean scent of rain hovered in the air and glistened in the leaves. She breathed deep as they turned away from the driveway and walked through a partially visible track that meandered through long, spiky grass, and wattle trees that glowed golden with flowers. Eucalyptus trees with white trunks towered overhead, their canopies hiding much of the sky until grass and trees gave way to a dozen large rocks.

Mackenzie guided her to a flat boulder at the edge of a cliff face. Taking off his jacket and placing it on the still damp rock surface, they sat down, his arm moving around her waist, and her head coming to rest on his shoulder.

In silence they watched the vague glow of dawn give way to a spectacular golden-orange sunrise. As light filled the air, she looked over the sweeping, endless valley of olive green sprinkled generously with the golden orbs of wattle flowers.

A small flock of brightly colored king parrots flew past, their shrill calls quickly fading away even as a magpie warbled into glorious morning song somewhere nearby in the trees.

"What do you think of the view?" he asked.

"It's spectacular." She pulled away to look at him fully. "I never took you for a romantic."

He cocked a dark brow. "Many women would argue being taken out for dinners and social events is romantic."

"That's because it's not also part of their job description."

"You don't enjoy your work?"

She shrugged, but he was too perceptive by far to imagine the casual gesture echoed her true feelings. "I think it's fair to say the novelty and gloss wore off some time ago."

"Then why don't you walk away?"

She managed a smile. "One day soon I intend to do just that."

"If it's money you need—"

Her smile faded and her spine snapped straight. "No. I don't need any man to step in and save me. But thank you anyway."

"So what *is* it you need then, Scarlet?" He shook his head. "Can I even ask that from you when I don't even know your real name?"

"Honestly, I don't need anything." She was doing just fine on her own. She blinked up at him. He didn't need to know her name. No client did. "And just so you know ... you don't give away too much about yourself either." She swept a hand out in the general direction of the cabin they'd left behind. "No photos. No keepsakes."

"So you're interested in my personal life?"

She swallowed back denial. He wasn't stupid. In fact, he was one of the most astute men she'd ever met. Maybe that was why he hadn't given up on her. He'd seen through her guise of not wanting to be with him. She bit her bottom lip and said evasively, "I just found it odd, that's all."

Placing an outspread hand behind him, he leaned back. He looked casual, but she sensed his mind was changing gears, pushing to know more. "In that case ... what is it you want to know?" he asked.

She looked out over the sweeping valley, barely taking any of it in. All her attention remained on the man beside her. "I want to know why you're so driven. What makes you tick? Why do you prefer paying call girls instead of forming a relationship with someone—"

"Whoa, one question at a time," he said with mock humor. He too turned to look over the valley, but he probably saw as little as she did when his face grew serious. "I guess I'm driven because I was brought up with very little, and went without a lot for too many years."

She nodded. She'd been right in guessing his upbringing had been vastly different to the lifestyle he now lived.

He twisted to face her. "Your turn."

She mentally shrank from his steady regard. Telling a client anything personal was wrong on so many levels, yet a deeper part of her stretched toward him, eager to share a little something of herself. "What do you want to know?"

"I want to know about your family."

She looked away. Why hadn't he asked about her call girl life, like any other male on the planet would have? That he was interested in the real girl behind the paid seductress created an even bigger crack in her defenses. "I'm the eldest of three girls. My younger sisters are identical twins and studying at university."

"Really?" he mused aloud, evidently fascinated by the breadcrumbs she tossed his way. "I bet your mother found plenty of grey in her hair when her twin daughters hit puberty together."

She hid a sad smile, though she sensed he perceived her every emotion. "No, any greys in the hair would have been mine." She sighed, and turned back his way, rueful now of the physical divide between them. "Our mother died when I was eighteen and the twins were thirteen."

His eyes softened. "I'm so sorry. Your father—"

"Walked out on us long before my mother passed away."

Understanding fell over his face, but it was the undertones of sympathy in his voice she couldn't take. "You felt as though you had no choice but to become a call girl."

She squeezed her eyes closed for a moment, fighting to regain some semblance of composure. The conversation was getting way too personal, way too fast. She had to remember they shared nothing more than amazing chemistry. She had to remember he was just another client. She pushed to her feet. "Not everything in life is that black or white."

He looked up. "So you're in the grey category?" His tone indicated she could never be that bland. In fact, his tone indicated she was some glorious, multi-colored rainbow full of glitter and life. Much like the king parrots that had flown past earlier.

She shook off the foolish thought. "You can't evaluate everyone with your analytical mind. Sometimes pieces of a puzzle aren't meant to fit."

He stood too, and it was her turn to look up. Damn he was tall, his presence sharply forbidding. He might be lean and hard, but he had more strength than any other man she'd known. It wasn't just physical strength either. His emotional and mental strength were uncompromising, even a little ruthless. Little wonder he was one of Australia's wealthiest men.

His dark eyes flashed. "If you were some boring puzzle, do you think I'd be half as interested? You intrigue me in a hundred different ways." He scrubbed a hand over his face. "God help me, even if I *could* fit all your pieces together, I'd still want you."

Need pulled her belly in every direction. But she had to keep her guard up and remember she was paid to be with him. She needed to revert to her professional persona. "I hope you'll always want me," she said huskily.

A pity he wasn't impressed, not one bit. His expletive touched a nerve deep inside her, as though he truly despaired he'd ever reach the real her. If only he realized her career was the farthest thing from her mind whenever she was with him. If only he knew how much she wished they'd met under different circumstances.

Dragging a hand over his face, he pulled in a steadying breath and said, "Drop the act, Scarlet. We've gone past all that now."

Her chin tilted. "Not according to my bank account."

If her words stung or served to remind him of their working relationship, his shuttered stare didn't let on. Instead he pulled out his cell and said, "You know, you're right, I don't have any photos. Maybe now is as good a time as any to take some and plaster them over the walls of my cabin."

When he finally lowered his cell phone camera after she'd endured at least a dozen different selfies with him, she asked drily, "Now what?"

He grinned. "Now we pack a picnic breakfast, and go for a hike."

~

Scarlet helped fill a basket with strawberries, exotic cheeses, crackers and a bottle of champagne that was warm thanks to the power outage. And all the while she admired the way Mackenzie's jeans fitted snugly to his butt and his thighs, and lovingly outlined his crotch.

Hell he could wear a sack and she'd still be aware of his taut physique. He was built like an athlete. Tall, lean and honed. She swallowed. He had the stamina of an athlete too.

He turned to her then, picnic basket in one hand and the other held out for her. "Ready?"

She nodded. "Sure." Though she had a feeling nowhere could be as impressive as the sunrise and sweeping views he'd shown her earlier that morning.

He led her back outside and along another track that veered down a sharp incline studded with shale and rocks. She was glad of Mackenzie's firm grip on the steeper, trickier parts of the path. Unlike sex and running, her thigh muscles weren't used to this type of a workout.

Thirty minutes later the track abruptly leveled out. Gum trees and grass trees gave way to a tiny valley, where a pool of water was fed by a waterfall that cascaded over rocks at least a hundred feet overhead. The scent of damp and eucalyptus filled the air, while the dull roar of water crashing onto the rocks below filled her ears.

Mackenzie placed the champagne bottle in the cold pool of water before he unfurled a picnic blanket and set the basket on top. He sat and reached for her, tugging her down to sit between his legs, the basket beside them.

She leaned against his chest, loving the rippling of his muscles against her back with his every movement, loving his warmth and familiar spiced scent.

"You must be starving," he said close to her ear, sending tingles down her spine, even as he reached inside the basket for a strawberry and placed it in her mouth. A burst of cool sweetness filled her mouth, and he chuckled at her gurgles of delight.

"Want another one?" he asked.

She nodded. "Yes, please."

She opened her mouth to the plump, juicy fruit, and he put a hand beneath her chin and tilted her head back, leaning down to kiss her lips and blot away residual juice. She closed her eyes, sighing against his mouth, his soft yet firm lips. His tender skill.

He pulled back and her eyelashes fluttered open to see his dark, gleaming eyes. "They taste almost as good as you," he said huskily.

Her heart flip-flopped, her blood thickening as yearning pulled through her veins. What she would have done to have met a man like Mackenzie outside her work. Men might see her as sex on a stick, but she had so many other needs too.

She dressed to please her clients, but fashion held no real interest to her. In fact, she much preferred her sneakers and exercise gear, or her sweats and oversized shirts.

She also preferred cooking for her sisters over dining out at fancy restaurants. She loved cutting up salads and making stir-fries, or baking her latest creation while her sisters giggled at the most recent gossip about everyday people in their everyday lives.

Probably because nothing about her own life was normal. She was as far removed from normal as one could get. People might embrace her while she kept her profession secret, but the moment she was exposed she'd become an outcast, a piece of lint on society. Only those men who could afford her would appreciate anything about her.

Even Danni and Tina had no idea where she worked, believing her to be a receptionist with a hard taskmaster of a boss who expected her to travel at the drop of a hat. Her sisters had always been wrapped up in their own lives and their own troubles, the twin thing ensuring their thoughts centered on one another.

And that's the way Scarlet wanted it to stay. Her sisters might have lost their mother at way too young an age, but at least they'd been spared from the harshness of life she'd experienced. At least they were able to take for granted their finances and lack of responsibilities.

Mackenzie placed another strawberry in her mouth, but this time she barely tasted its sweetness.

Better that she dressed to impress and put on social airs and graces while pretending interest in her latest client's needs. Better that she ate at expensive restaurants where the portion size was never enough to fill the hole in her belly. Better that she fucked men with enough acting skills to keep them coming back for more, while inside she shriveled a little more each time.

Heat tingled across her face. Better for everyone but her.

Chapter Five

Mackenzie sampled one of the strawberries, but she could feel his gaze on her. "Is something wrong?" he asked softly.

She forced herself to hold his gaze, and not admit to all the self-doubts bulldozing through her defenses. "Nothing I can't handle."

His gaze searched hers, shrewd and assessing. "You don't have to be strong all the time."

She shook her head. "I don't know how to be weak."

Even before her mother had died she'd been the strong one. She'd held her mother's hand when overnight she'd become a single mother. She'd held her hand again and watched as her mother withered away from cancer. Then held her sisters' hands at their mother's funeral, where few mourners attended.

Mackenzie nodded. "One of the many reasons I'm drawn to you." She blinked, and he added, "We're survivors in a dog-eat-dog world."

It was her turn to search his stare. "What was your childhood like?"

A shadow moved like a cloud behind his eyes. "It wasn't great."

"Oh?" she prompted.

He exhaled. "My mother was a victim of spousal abuse." He squeezed his eyes shut, his features taut with memory. He opened his eyes, uncertainty stamped across his face before he concluded softly, "She died at the hands of my father."

Her heart wrenched for him, the little boy who'd undoubtedly seen far too much at too young an age. Little wonder he carried so many wounds inside. She turned around, placing her knees on either side of his hips as her hands outlined his jaw. "I know words can't take away what's been done, but I'm sorry, Mack."

He looked up at her with weariness tugging at his mouth. At least now she understood why the windows to his soul were shuttered so tight. He had a past he didn't want to dwell on. A past she'd bet wounded and scraped like daggers to the heart.

He placed his hands over hers, as though drawing from her touch. His voice was hoarse when he said, "You're right, nothing can take away the past. I only wish you didn't understand so well what it is to feel the loss of a mother."

She leaned towards him, kissing him with a tenderness that belied their working relationship. Sharing an intimacy and understanding that she'd never granted to another man. She'd always felt an affinity with Mackenzie, had been drawn to him from the very start. Like two lost souls who'd found one another and couldn't let go.

She jerked back, biting her bottom lip even as she fought off a surge of panic. She was *not* falling for this man! He was a client, one with internal scars that might never heal. And right now all they had in common was a past that haunted them both.

"I didn't scare you off?" he asked, his voice mock-humorous but his stare all too serious.

She shook her head. "I don't scare away that easily."

Liar! Everything about Mackenzie terrifies you. And you've already tried running from him once.

His smile seemed forced. "C'mon, let's have a swim."

They pushed to their feet and Scarlet was aware of the distance between them even as they stripped off their clothes and stood in all their naked glory. A breeze rippled across the water, saturating the air with moisture from the falls and pulling free some wisps of her hair.

Mackenzie clearly didn't believe her. Probably already realized she'd lied to him in the past about not having feelings for him.

But once they slid into the cold lagoon, whatever layers he'd mentally surrounded himself with appeared to slowly fall away as they paddled over to the waterfall's splash-off. She laughed at the spray hammering their faces, and Mackenzie's smile was real this time as he watched her delight.

"I've never seen a woman so damn beautiful," he murmured huskily, swimming toward her and turning her into his arms so that he shielded her from the worst of the spray. And somehow treading water he managed to kiss her before they slowly sank and had to kick back up, gasping for air and laughing at their own stupidity.

She splashed him then, full in the face. And he roared with pretend retaliation even as she turned and kicked furiously away to outswim him. She lasted no more than a couple of seconds before his hand clasped her ankle and he yanked her back. But this time he stood while she spluttered and gasped for breath, the solid ground underfoot too far out of her reach.

She had no choice than to wind her legs around his hips, his cock pressing thick and hard against her belly. She wrapped her arms around his nape, his stare holding hers even as their mouths merged together as one in a kiss that was as fierce as the feelings they'd been holding back for so long.

She rubbed against him, and he groaned into her mouth, his cock jerking in response before he pulled his mouth from hers and asked throatily, "Ever done it in a stream before?"

She giggled. "I can't say that I have."

His eyes glowed, and she inhaled sharply when he touched her between the petals of her sex, his finger sliding deep into her warmth. She shivered, aroused beyond words when he began to rhythmically push in and out. She rocked against him and he pushed two fingers inside, his eyes not once leaving hers as he urged her to a place only he knew how to take her.

The moment she wondered if she could possibly take anymore, he touched the bud of her clit and she shattered around his fingers, her body shuddering with rapture as she moaned out his name.

He covered the sound with his mouth, kissing away her vocal ecstasy. She leaned into him, sated and weak, and drawing his oxygen into her lungs.

He pulled back, his eyes glinting with need, even as he murmured, "We have company."

She stiffened in his arms, and he grinned at her reaction. She tore her stare away from him to view a middle-aged couple approaching along the track, before they set up a blanket and towels just as few feet from their own.

"What do we do now?" she hissed.

His grin widened. "Don't tell me you're shy."

She glared. "I'm not going to give them a free show, if that's what you mean."

It was one thing to flaunt her naked body to a client, quite another to reveal it to some unsuspecting bystanders.

He turned her around, so that she faced away from the couple. Clasping her hand, he pressed it against his rock-hard groin and drawled, "It could be worse ... you could also have a raging hard-on to conceal."

She pressed her lips together to bite back a giggle. A pity a snort escaped instead. "Isn't the water too cold?"

It couldn't be any later than nine in the morning. The sun's fierce heat hadn't had a chance to warm up the water. They'd freeze if they lingered in it for too much longer.

He shrugged. "Try telling my dick that."

She chewed her bottom lip. "We're in quite the predicament then, aren't we?"

He shook his head. "Only if we let it be."

She frowned, not liking where the conversation seemed to be headed. "What do you mean?"

"I mean ... let's just get this over with."

Shock rendered her speechless when he lifted her against his chest and then waded out of the stream. She pressed an arm against her breasts and squeezed her legs together, trying for modesty but undoubtedly failing.

The middle-aged couple looked up and it was hard to tell which of the two looked more stunned. Scarlet smothered another bout of giggles. Their expressions were priceless! And right then she didn't much care that the man on the ground boldly eyed her off, or that his partner took her fill of Mackenzie's taut nakedness.

Only after Mackenzie put her down and shielded her with the picnic blanket so she could dress, did the full irony hit. She made a living using her body like a musician used an instrument. Yet the moment no paycheck was exchanged, she'd become as shy and virginal as a blushing bride.

Mackenzie pulled on his clothes too before he grabbed the basket and picnic blanket and they strolled past the goggle-eyed couple. He nodded at them. "Beautiful day for a swim."

Scarlet grinned and retrieved the champagne bottle from the cool water. Once they were out of sight of the couple, Mackenzie led her off the track and placed the picnic blanket underneath some shade. He uncorked the bottle and offered it to her. She grinned and took a swig, before handing it back to him.

She couldn't help but admire his throat as it contracted as he swallowed, his neck tanned and strong. And the way his long fingers splayed around the bottle, his big hand dwarfing it. She knew all too well how good his hands felt around her breasts, his clever fingers plucking her nipples, before taking charge of her pussy and making her come over and over.

He handed her the bottle once again and she accepted it with a sigh. She took another big sip and enjoyed the decadent bubbles that slid down her throat. In many ways it felt as though she should be paying Mackenzie for the pleasure of his company. He always made sure she enjoyed herself. Always made sure she got as much pleasure as he did.

She handed it back to him with a contented sigh. "Privacy at last."

"You're such a contradiction," he murmured.

She wiped her mouth. "Oh? How so?"

"You attract men with your body like bees to a honeypot, and yet in many ways you're a prude." He shook his head and grinned. "Somehow you only manage to fascinate me all the more."

She raised a brow. "That's my aim."

His eyes darkened. "You're not even thinking about your work right now, Scarlet, so don't try and tell me otherwise."

She blinked, and then nodded. "You're right ... I'm not. I enjoy being myself with you."

Taking one more swig of the champagne, he passed it to her pointedly. "I don't know any high-class escorts who'd stoop to drinking from a bottle like this."

She paused, the bottle at her lips. "Are you calling me cheap?"

He chuckled. "Hardly cheap, my love."

My love?

Her heart fluttered with yearning. But she mentally shook off any more irrational fantasies, and drank deep, belching a little as the bubbles hit her belly fast. She grinned. "Excuse me, then."

His grin lit up his eyes. "It's nice seeing you this relaxed."

She shrugged. "I've just been exposed in front of two strangers. There's nothing left to be uptight about."

His grin widened, and he dug in the basket and brought out the cheese and crackers. "At least it's given them something to talk about for a while."

It was Scarlet's turn to grin. "I suspect they might be doing a whole lot more than talking right now."

It was only after Mackenzie handfed her crackers and cheese, and they finished off what was left of the wine, that they decided to head back to the cabin. Scarlet felt as though she was walking on air, and it wasn't just from the champagne. Being with Mackenzie was exciting and intense, emotions that seemed amplified the more time she spent with him.

Little wonder she'd run scared from him in the past. He threatened everything about her way of life, made her question herself and all the 'what could have beens'. Suddenly she didn't feel very light anymore. A weight settled on her shoulders and made the rest of the hike somehow oppressive.

She sucked in a steadying breath. She had to revert back to her call girl role, had to reinforce just exactly why she was here and what she was doing. And that certainly didn't include heart-to-heart chats and being drawn close to a man who was her client.

At some stage over the weekend she'd not just stepped over the line in the sand, she'd gone into danger territory, a minefield of hope, yearning, need and desire. She needed to concentrate on the latter and forget all the rest. *Had* to if she wanted to keep her heart intact.

But she managed to keep up a half decent banter even once they arrived back at the cabin. He placed the basket on the dining table and she helped him unpack the few pieces of cutlery and dishes they'd used.

Five minutes later she'd dried the last container and placed it back into the cupboard. She glanced sideward at Mackenzie as he wiped off the sink. It was funny how the everyday task of cleaning felt so right, so normal. Like they were a married couple with a normal, everyday life.

Not a client and his expensive call girl.

He looked up. "Everything okay?"

She dropped the tea towel and turned to face him with a smile. "Just thinking how overpriced I am as a cleaner."

His lips curled. "Yeah, I guess you are."

It really was beyond time to remind him once again what she was here for. Her blood warmed and her nipples tightened even before she leisurely pulled her shirt over her head, and unclipped her lacy bra. "I could think of some things that might be more worth your while."

He stilled, his eyes soaking her in like his cloth had soaked in the dishwater. "Is that right?" he asked throatily.

She nodded, and slipped free the button on her jeans. As she pulled the zipper down with a rasp, she added, "Much more enjoyable too."

Mackenzie didn't move. But going by the swelling in his jeans and his glittering stare, he was too busy enjoying the show.

She stepped out of her jeans and slid her thong ever so slowly down her thighs, bending low and showing him her curves that he paid so much to touch and fuck. She didn't work out and exercise daily just for the joy of it. She was nubile, fit and healthy, an athlete and a performer. And she was damn good at her job.

Tossing her thong aside, she slowly straightened. Watching him watch her, pride and desire filled her in equal measure. Pleasing a man was her goal, and Mackenzie was beyond pleased. His eyes all but burned for her.

She slid her fingertips up her sides and then under her breasts, cupping them and gently kneading. When Mackenzie stepped wide and leaned against the table, before sliding a hand inside his jeans, her pussy immediately moistened.

She slid her hand down her own body, past the flat plane of her belly and between the petals of her sex. As Mackenzie stroked his shaft, she slid a finger deep into her wet warmth.

He groaned at the visual, his jaw tight and his arousal pushing against his jeans. "That's it, baby," he gritted, "make yourself come."

She might be paid to do his every sexual bidding, but there was nothing mercenary behind her need to do just as he asked. She massaged her clit rhythmically, her breasts becoming heavy and her nipples tight, her blood thick and warm through her veins.

When Mackenzie unzipped his fly and reminded her he'd gone commando, her mouth watered. His shaft was big, thick and ribbed with blue veins, pre-cum already seeping from its head.

Damn, could a man be any more physically perfect? She rubbed harder, faster. She was two seconds and two steps away from climbing onto him and filling herself with his cock.

She cried out, toes curling and breaths shuddering as she yielded to an intense, sharp orgasm.

Mackenzie's eyes glowed, and he stroked his cock in faster pulls. But it was only when her soft cries of pleasure had died off that he stepped toward her, clasped her waist and lifted her onto the bench.

"Legs over my shoulders," he commanded hoarsely.

"But you haven't come yet," she said, breathless and yielding. He hadn't at the falls either.

His stare burned with intensity. "Not yet, no. I'm saving that for when I'm deep inside you. But first I need to taste you like I need my next damn breath."

His talk stimulated her almost as much as spreading her legs apart and opening herself to his glittering gaze did. It was beyond erotic to place her legs over his corded shoulders, his skin warm and satin-smooth, his muscles shifting and flexing with every movement.

It was even more erotic watching his dark head move between her thighs, his bristles scraping her tender skin and his mouth latching onto her clit. She arched back and moaned in delight as he pleasured her, licking and sucking, using his teeth, lips and tongue to taste her. Tease and torment her.

Until she leaned back onto her elbows and squeezed her eyes closed as a kaleidoscope of color swept through her, and she quivered and gasped at yet another climax.

He pulled back and licked his lips, satisfaction glinting in his eyes. "I love tasting you. Almost as much as I love making you come."

She blinked, and said huskily, "It's your turn now."

His teeth gleamed white, his lazy smile somehow revealing his anticipation. She slid her legs off his shoulders and he stepped back, giving her room to move off the bench and kneel in front of him. She looked up as she clasped his cock, holding his dark stare as she leaned forward and licked the salty, sticky essence from his cock.

Mackenzie wondered if it was possible to view a more erotic sight. Scarlet on her knees and naked to his hungry eyes. Her mouth wrapped around his dick. Then she licked him again, before sucking his shaft deep into her mouth in one wet, warm slide.

He groaned, his balls tightening as she began the up and down movement with her skilled lips and tongue. Her sharp little teeth grazed his sensitive skin at intermittent moments, a pleasure–pain that made him impossibly harder.

It was enough that he had the best view of her tits that bounced pertly with every up and down motion. But then she released his dick from her mouth and pushed her breasts together around his cock. His breath hissed, his seed two seconds away from pearling over her pale-as-lily skin.

He shook his head. He'd only been bare inside her pussy once, and it'd been heaven. He wanted to experience that again. No condom. No protection. Just his sensitized cock plunging into her tight, wet cunt.

He clasped her upper arms and she straightened, her lips rosy and her eyes slumberous with need. "I need to be inside you now," he grated, even as he lifted her against his chest and strode to his bedroom. "And I'm not going to be gentle."

Her excited mewl turned him on even more. Placing her on the end of the bed, he commanded hoarsely, "Turn around."

She did as he asked, her pale back and buttocks facing his way as he clasped his cock and guided it to the lips of her gorgeous pussy. In one motion he thrust forward, his cock sinking deep, her inner muscles grasping and pulling, her guttural moan joining his own.

He clasped her shoulders as he retreated. When he sank deep on the second stroke, he clasped a handful of her hair and tugged her head back. Just the way she liked it.

Fuck. Just the way they both liked it.

Her tits bounced with every in and out, the slapping of their flesh sounding loud in the quiet, the musky scent of their union filling his nose like an aphrodisiac.

Not that he needed it. He was balls deep in Scarlet's hot pussy and he was doing everything not to explode. To savor and enjoy the ride for as long as humanly possible.

Scarlet hadn't read the memo. His strokes in and out were getting hard and fast when her inner muscles grabbed at him and she came with a half-strangled moan. All but milking his seed right out of him.

He bellowed out something incomprehensible. It could have been her name. Hell, it could have been Latin. He was thrown into a higher plane where only pleasure existed. Where nothing mattered but utter, exquisite bliss.

Where only he and Scarlet existed.

Chapter Six

Scarlet lay on her side, her head burrowed into Mackenzie's neck. She breathed in his spiced vanilla maleness, feeling relaxed and sated, but aware of how little she still knew about her lover ... her client. He'd given her the vaguest details about himself while she'd rattled on way too much about her personal life.

His breath warmed her head before his lips pressed against her brow and he murmured, "Everything okay?"

She crooked her head back, meeting his warm stare. Damn, she'd never seen him so laid-back and at ease. She liked seeing him this way ... a lot. This relaxed side of him was a far call from the arrogant, controlled and masterful man most people knew. She sighed. "You've learned quite a lot about me now, yet I still know very little about you."

His warmth faded a few degrees. "I haven't learned your name."

She frowned. "You know that's confidential."

He arched a brow. "And you know any information can be bought for a price."

"You wouldn't—"

"You'd be surprised what I would do for you," he murmured. Tucking a piece of hair behind her ear, he sighed and said, "Fine ... Scarlet. I won't uncover your real name."

Why did she get the feeling he was simply biding his time? If he wanted something, he wouldn't give in. He'd fight until he got it. His various businesses all around the world were proof of that. And Lord only knew he'd fought hard enough to get her away from Amos, and then to have her for himself this weekend.

She cleared her throat, focusing on her earlier question before he skilfully got her sidetracked again. "So you never answered my question."

"About?" he hedged.

"About how little I know you."

"What is it exactly you want to know?"

She pushed aside professional courtesy. She might have always kept her nose out of her clients' personal lives, but at some point she and Mackenzie had gone past that line drawn in the sand.

Her chin tilted. "Why is it you prefer call girls instead of forming a relationship with one woman?"

He stiffened ever so slightly, but he didn't gloss over the subject matter. "I've had plenty of relationships in the past. But it was with women who wanted more from me than what I was willing to give."

She blinked. He didn't do commitment. Just the same as her father.

His stare heated. "Women who weren't you."

Her breath caught. What was he saying? That he actually *wanted* commitment with her? Wanted something more permanent?

Treacherous yearning bloomed in her chest, even as she breathed, "You don't mean that."

"Why would I lie?"

Because that was what most men she knew did. They pretended they wanted to settle down and have a family, except they didn't want the noose of children, a wife, and responsibilities. They wanted a no-strings-attached, beautiful woman in their bed. And most were willing to pay good money for that fantasy.

She felt lightheaded, balancing on a tightrope between desperate hope and disbelief. But she was saved from answering when Mackenzie's phone abruptly rang out, loud and strident.

He grunted annoyance. "This conversation isn't over." He kissed her brow again and turned to reach for his phone on the side table. His hoarse voice filled the quiet. "Emma, what's wrong?" He sat, his whole body taut, tense, while emotion she'd never heard before thickened his voice. "Christ, Em, how many times did I ask you to leave that sack of shit and move in with me?"

Scarlet's throat dried, her pulse thudding and her whole body going still as she drank in his every word like the world's greatest masochist.

He dragged a hand through his hair, his voice strained. "Yeah, well, I haven't exactly hidden my feelings, have I?"

Scarlet squeezed her eyes closed. So much for her being the only woman for him. Evidently this Emma had a stranglehold on his heart. A woman he'd obviously assumed was out of his reach. She swallowed. It sure sounded like she was in his reach now.

She pushed away the deep ache in her chest. She'd experienced abandonment and knew better than to let her heart rule her head. Lesson learned. She should be happy for him. Hell, she was only his paid fuck. Happily ever afters might happen to women like Brandy—Kate—but they sure as hell didn't happen to people like her.

He turned his back fully to her, the distance between them wider than a chasm. "Em, you *have* to leave him." He sounded anguished, every molecule of his attention on the other woman. "Look, stay where you are, I'll come get you."

His knuckles whitened on the phone at whatever she said. He shook his head. "Just ... let me look after you."

Scarlet's heart shrank even more. She'd been a fool to give Mackenzie access to a part of her she'd always kept off-limits. It was her own fault that hurt, pain and loss, now seeped through her. She should have known better. She'd gone against her instincts and broken too many rules for him. Told him too much about herself. Opened her heart and mind to a man who paid for nothing but sex.

How had she imagined things would be different with him? She blew out a stricken, but silent breath, then sat and swung her legs to the side of the bed. It was clearly past time to get dressed and pack her bag. The weekend with her client had just been cut short.

Fifteen minutes later she sat silent and subdued as he drove back the way they'd come, at a speed that might have frightened her under any other circumstances. Instead her emotions were a tangled, fractured mess, though she put on her best professional front. She could never let him see just how much she'd let him into her life.

She glanced at him. His face was taut, lips compressed, his mind clearly on the other woman. She ignored the ache that seemed to deepen with each mile closer to home. With each minute that Mackenzie sank deeper into his own thoughts about his lover and away from her.

She sighed. "She must be special."

He glanced her way, his mind still far away as he focused on her words. He nodded absently. "She is. And deserves far better than the man she chose."

So Emma had desired some other man over Mackenzie? The woman surely mustn't be right in the head. She had a feeling Mackenzie would give his all to the right woman. But maybe now he had that chance with Emma. Maybe they'd find happiness.

She hoped so. He was a good man and deserved someone special. But though she wanted to congratulate him, the words turned to ashes on her tongue. She couldn't pretend the idea of him with another woman didn't burn her all the way to her marrow. Couldn't pretend right then she didn't wish she was Emma.

Couldn't pretend that Mackenzie's attentions hadn't broken down her defenses.

When she'd asked him why he chose call girls over a relationship, she never expected him to prove otherwise. Never expected him to be in love with someone unavailable.

Someone who was evidently now all too available.

Scarlet had nothing more to say, nothing that wouldn't sound false, empty. Instead she distracted herself by retrieving her cell phone from her bag and putting through a quick call to Maisey, asking for the town car to be waiting at the pickup point.

Mackenzie had paid her to do a job and she'd see it through to the end, no matter if inside her heart was breaking.

She ignored the madam's faintly accusatory tone. She already felt rejected and unwanted. She didn't need to feel even worse. She disconnected the call and tossed it back into her bag.

"Scarlet, I'm sorry."

She turned and faced Mackenzie, her professional mask in place. "Don't be sorry." That was the very last thing she wanted from him. "I earned a lot of money for doing very little. It's nothing but a win for me."

His jaw tightened. "Is that all you see in me—a bank balance?"

Her face burned. She refused to feel bad. "I'm not a call girl for the sheer love of sex alone."

He stared straight ahead. "No. I guess you're not." He scraped a hand over his face. "I had hoped your feelings might have come into it though."

She gritted her teeth. He wanted her heart even as he ran back to another woman. His arrogance was beyond astounding. But so many men paid to hear whatever boosted their ego, just the same as they paid to satisfy their sexual urges.

But she'd thought Mackenzie was different. Honorable. She pressed a splayed hand to her chest. Guess she should be glad he wasn't one of her clients with a wife and children at home.

"I care about you," she conceded softly, though the truth was like sawdust in her mouth. "You're an amazing man, and a wonderful client."

He turned to her. “I’d planned to step up our relationship this weekend.”

Until Emma had called and thrown a spanner in the works? Until Emma had reminded him just exactly who he wanted?

Certainly not an escort.

Men fucked call girls, not married them.

Why had it taken her so long to realize Mackenzie was just the same as every other man she’d known?

He pulled into the service station, his face relaxing just a little on seeing the town car that would safely take her home. She hid a sad smile. At least he hadn’t completely abandoned his integrity ... completely abandoned her.

He climbed out and opened the passenger door, and held her hand as she alighted. His stare brushed over her face before he leaned forward and kissed her lightly on the lips. “I’ll be in touch soon, okay?”

She stared up at him, reading his expression that was torn between lingering with her and racing back to Emma. Sadness welled up inside her. She shook her head. “I won’t hold you to that.”

He frowned, his eyes darkening. “Scarlet—”

“Just go, Mackenzie.” She’d never call him Mack again. “Go to Emma.”

His frown deepened, even as he shut the passenger door and said, “You don’t get rid of me that easily.”

He didn’t leave until he’d escorted her to the town car and watched her climb into its back seat. She kept her head high, even when he gave her a nod then turned and strode back to his SUV, its tires squealing as he took off.

Only then did she lean her head against the back seat, weariness falling over her like a heavy blanket. Her heart ached, her head tight with tension. She closed her eyes. She’d walked away from Mackenzie the first time because her heart had been at risk. She’d been a fool to think the second time wouldn’t be any more painful.

A tear leaked out the corner of her eye, and she didn't have the energy to wipe it away. She had to walk away from Mackenzie for good this time.

Or risk losing everything for him.

Chapter Seven

Mackenzie arrived at his sister's home in record time. Killing the SUV's ignition, he was at the front door of the sprawling mansion not even a minute later. He didn't knock; instead he thrust the door open and strode inside the cold, white, soul-sucking ambience of the house.

"Emma!"

His voice echoed eerily. He turned around, his heart thudding with adrenaline and squeezing with fear even as he was propelled back to the powerless little boy all those years ago.

"You ugly, spineless whore!"

Mackenzie pressed his hands even tighter to his ears, but nothing could block out his father's yelling, and his mother's terrified whimpering, just as nothing would convince him that his father was right.

His mother was beautiful, and her only weakness was his big, mean father.

He'd do whatever he had to so that his mother wouldn't get hurt again.

His heart hammered even before he pushed his bedroom door open fully and stepped into the family room. "Leave her alone."

His father shoved his mother to the floor, before turning his furious, drunken stare his way. "What did you say, boy?"

Mackenzie trembled inside, but he did his best to hide his fear when he said even louder, "Leave her alone!"

His dad's red eyes glinted with equal parts respect and betrayal. The latter won out. "You little piece of shit, you're telling *me* what to do in my own house, with my own wife?"

Mackenzie's hands fisted, though he was as good as useless against his towering, enraged father. "If you don't want us in the house, then we'll leave."

He thought he could hear his sister's whimpering sobs from her bedroom next to his own. He quivered. Emma was afraid for him, and that made him even more scared.

"No-one leaves this house, leaves me, without my saying so." His father staggered toward him, forearms bunched and hands clenched. Mackenzie stood his ground, even when his father's fist lifted. He wouldn't show him fear, wouldn't give him the satisfaction.

The blow knocked him off his feet and into the air, before blackness fell over him like a curtain.

~

"Mack, I'm here."

His focus came back to the present, his heart rate immediately settling back into rhythm on seeing Emma paused halfway down the stairs. He dragged a hand over his face, for just a moment blocking the visual of his sister's condition. It didn't stop sorrow from filling him to the brim.

One of her eyes was bruised and swollen half-shut. Both eyes were red-rimmed and shadowed with fatigue, not to mention dull and empty. Her once beautiful golden hair was lank and knotted, her skin pale and her body fragile. She looked as if she'd fall over in a breeze.

"What did that bastard do to you this time?" he snarled.

She shook her head. "It wasn't his fault. I shouldn't have argued—"

"Listen to yourself," he gritted out. He refused to shout at her, to make her fear him as much as her evil, politician husband. "You're making the same damn excuses our mother used to make for our father ... before he hit her one too many times."

As much as it half-killed them both to think back on those times, Emma needed to hear the truth. She needed to break the chain of domestic violence that bound her like manacles to her husband, Stewart.

"Stop!" she hissed, arms folding like hovering birds in front of her. "Stewart is nothing like our dad."

Mackenzie took the stairs, and then stilled in front of her. "Isn't he?"

She dropped her eyes. "I love him."

He exhaled heavily. How had his sister come to this fucked up point in her life? She deserved so much better. Deserved a normal life. Deserved a man who loved her. "Emma, we both know you'd be better off broke and on the streets than living with the monster that is your husband."

She shook her head. "The elections are coming up next month—"

"Screw the elections!" he gritted. Reining back his emotions, he gently clasped her elbow and guided her back upstairs. "Pack your bags. If you really must live with someone successful and rich, then you'll live with me."

Emma cried then, tears falling down her bruised and swollen face, her split lip. Her terror at even considering his proposal rolled off her in waves as she said shakily, "Stewart will find me!"

Mackenzie felt bile rise from his belly. How could his sister be so goddamn blind? Had she forgotten the memories that still haunted him every single day? Or was she living the only way she knew how?

One thing was for sure. She was fearful of her husband's retribution for leaving him. She was fearful for her life.

A vein throbbed to life in his jaw. Stewart wouldn't get anywhere near Emma. "I'll hire round-the-clock guards and beef up security. You'll never have to worry about him again."

She looked up at him and shook her head. "I don't want anyone else to protect me but you, Mack. I don't feel safe with any other man."

He nodded. Of course she had major trust issues with men. Hell, she had even before their father had been dragged away from their dead mother by the authorities.

But even if he worked from the office in his penthouse, he couldn't stay right by her side twenty-four-seven. He'd have no choice but to station bodyguards around the hotel and outside his penthouse elevator. And if the lowlife scum that was Emma's husband somehow found a way to his penthouse ... well, Mackenzie wouldn't repress an inner violence just waiting to escape.

His lips thinned. Perhaps the apple didn't fall far from the tree after all.

It wasn't until after he'd helped Emma pack and carried her bags out to his SUV, that he wondered what Scarlet had thought about the weekend that'd been cut so short. He sighed. He'd had such big plans. But she'd understand his sister's safety and wellbeing was a priority.

He only wished he'd told Scarlet even a little so that she better understood the situation. Instead he'd been too wired up worrying about Emma. And possibly too used to shielding the truth because of Stewart's damn public image. Not that he gave a shit about Stewart. He only cared what the negative publicity would do to his sister.

But Scarlet had overheard at least some of his phone conversation. She'd undoubtedly put two and two together. The moment Emma had settled in and his doctor had visited to give her a thorough check-up, he'd see Scarlet again and explain some things.

His hands tightened on the steering wheel as he negotiated the city traffic. If he wanted Scarlet's trust he needed to be more open with her. She'd given him some insight into her own life, something that he knew was forbidden in her line of work. The least he could do was return the favor.

He only hoped his unintentional neglect hadn't pushed Scarlet away from him for good this time.

~

Claire pushed aside her salad and instead took a big gulp of her wine. It was a mistake coming here. She should have stayed home and wallowed in her misery, not met up with her friends for a late lunch.

Although she tried to enjoy the usual banter going on around her with her friends, Eloise, Natalie and Anna—otherwise known as Savannah, Tiffany and Candy—her heart wasn't in it. Not with her thoughts constantly straying to Mackenzie.

Had he and Emma made up yet? Had they made love?

She didn't realize she'd gasped until a soft hand landed on hers and three sets of eyes stared her way.

"Are you okay?" asked Anna gently, her hand tightening reassuringly and her hazel stare as gentle as a doe's. Claire blinked, all too aware Anna was still the angelic goddess she'd always been and somehow untarnished by the sex industry.

Claire cleared her throat and nodded, before glancing down at Anna's petite hand. Just how old was Anna anyway? She looked back up and managed a smile. "I'm okay, thanks."

Eloise snorted and flicked back a wedge of her gorgeous, inky-black hair. "Anna, you won't get anything personal from Claire. Her emotions are locked up tighter than a chastity belt. Even on her worst days she's Miss Cool, Calm and Collected."

If only they knew. She'd been nothing but an open book for Mackenzie, her heart worn on her sleeve. She'd ignored her better judgment and followed her heart instead of her head. She was only lucky she hadn't jumped headfirst into the deep end, or she'd be drowning even further in her own misery.

Natalie's considering, icy-blue stare lingered on her. Then she grinned and said, "I think this calls for a round of tequila shots!"

Eloise cheered, her free-spirited nature coming to the fore. "Let's get this party started!"

~

Claire walked into her house with a dozen shopping bags full of the sexy clothes she needed as a call girl. Lacy, barely there bras and thongs, corsets in cream and black, plunging dresses in various lengths, as well as strappy designer heels and thigh-high boots. None of it brought her any real joy. But what it did buy was her sisters' educations.

She dumped the bags on her table and pressed a hand to her roiling belly. She'd had one too many shots with the girls. They'd somehow interspersed their clothes shopping with drinking sessions, going into whatever bar they walked past.

There'd been a lot of bars. And a lot of shots.

She headed to the bathroom and peeled off her summery, floral print dress that cost an arm and a leg. Elegant and classy, she reminded herself. She couldn't go out in just any old T-shirt and jeans. She had a public image to uphold. Had to look good with the chance she might run into a past, present or future client. Those odds were greatly increased when she and her call girl friends got together.

She sighed. Not yet twenty-five years old and already she was looking forward to retiring from her profession. She turned on the taps and adjusted the temperature to hot, before stepping under the spray. But more than anything, she looked forward to having an ordinary, uncomplicated life.

She felt slightly better after a shower. Even more so after she'd dragged on old denim shorts and a faded grey T-shirt. Slipping her feet into an old pair of sneakers, she tied her hair up and walked out the front door.

Her smile was pained. Thanks to Mack, she had the rest of the afternoon off with full pay. It was time to lose herself in Mrs. Gracie's garden.

Chapter Eight

Mackenzie sat in his car with his hands clenched around the steering wheel. Indecision pulled him every which way. He'd parked just down the street from Scarlet's house, but his legs refused to obey his compulsion to get out, knock on Scarlet's door, then take her in his arms and make love to her for the rest of the day.

Not because he'd officially paid for her time. He wanted her because ... he wanted her.

He blew out a slow breath. If only the violence simmering inside him after seeing Emma's physical injuries hadn't given him second thoughts about Scarlet. Given him second thoughts about the woman he wanted more than anything else in the world.

What if he truly was like his father?

What if, in a moment of anger, he struck the woman who he wanted only to care for; to love and to hold? He scraped a hand over his face. In his mind, Scarlet was the woman he imagined as his future wife, the mother of his children.

But he couldn't help but ask himself if he was selfish to even consider dragging her into a life where his genetics might one day win out over his love for her.

Love.

He blew out a breath. When she'd left him the first time he'd dismissed the bitter ache within, imagined he'd forget her by losing himself in other women. He'd been a fool. Each woman only reminded him how much he wanted Scarlet back.

He'd only stayed away all those months because of her words, which had rung in his ears for weeks. He leaned his head back against his seat, her cool voice again echoing in his head like it was just yesterday.

I don't have feelings for you ... not the way you want me to.

She'd reopened a part of him that his father had tried to destroy. Peeled off the scab to his deepest wound.

He'd never wanted a woman more than he'd wanted Scarlet. He'd grown used to getting what he wanted, used to women hanging onto his every word and falling over themselves to date him.

Her rejection had been a kick in the guts and a smash to his ego, and it had taken him too long to ignore his hurt pride and go after her like he did everything else. But although he'd relished learning she did indeed have feelings for him, in some ways he wished he hadn't made that discovery.

If she loved him half as much as he loved her, would he be doing her a greater service in letting her go?

His belly cramped in rejection even as he reached for the ignition. About to fire up the engine, he watched as the door to Scarlet's house swung open and she stepped outside. His breath caught. God, she was gorgeous. Stunning. Her long, creamy legs were bared in little denim shorts, her tee hugging her slender curves and full breasts. Her hair was pulled up into its usual topknot, enhancing her gorgeous features. But this time her face was free of makeup, and she looked younger, almost virtuous.

He frowned. He had no idea of Scarlet's age. He swallowed. Fucking hell. He wanted to marry her, but he still knew very little about her. Hell, he could have dated her on her birthday and he wouldn't have known.

His stare followed her as she stepped onto the pathway and walked briskly up the street. He watched until she was nearly out of sight, before he started the car and eased it forward.

There was no harm in following her for a bit. At the very least, make sure she was okay. Except the moment she stepped through the gate of an old house, and then knocked on the door to have it opened by a good-looking young man, all his do-gooder instincts rushed out the window.

He pulled the car to the curb, every instinct on high alert. She might be a call girl, with God knew how many clients, but he couldn't deny it any longer. She. Was. His.

Claire was shocked to see who opened the door to Mrs. Gracie's home. "Bradley!" She stepped into his arms for a hug that was all friendship before looking up at him. Aside from a scruffy beard and his blond, tousled hair needing a cut, he'd hardly changed. "When did you get here?"

He grinned. "Just this morning. But if I had known you still visited Gran I would have been here much sooner."

Claire was aware of Bradley's infatuation, and maybe in another life she might have explored something more meaningful with him. But in this life, she had her profession, which pretty much wiped out any chance of a relationship. And even if that alone didn't destroy things, Mackenzie had taken away her desire to be with anyone else.

She shook her head and smiled wryly. "Still a charmer, I see."

He stepped back, his grin not quite so broad at her making light of his affections. "Come in. I'm sure Gran would love to see you too."

"Thanks."

Mrs. Gracie was in the kitchen, a smile creasing her already lined face. "Hello, dear. So nice to see you. And you're just in time for afternoon tea."

Bradley nodded. "It's a bit later than we intended, but my flight got delayed."

Mrs. Gracie slathered her scones with jam and cream, before placing them on a plate. Claire's belly rumbled. She'd barely touched her lunch when she'd met up with her friends, not to mention she'd had far too much to drink. Not the best combination. "Thank you, that'd be lovely."

Mrs. Gracie handed the plate of scones to her grandson, and gave Claire the tray with a teapot, milk, sugar and cups. "Go on out the back. I'm sure you and Bradley have lots to catch up on. I'll be out as soon as I freshen up."

Claire followed Bradley to the back patio, placing her tray next to his on the glass-topped table. He poured her a tea and she smiled thanks even as she took hold of a scone and bit deep. "Mmm." She closed her eyes. Little wonder Mrs. Gracie had won numerous awards for her baking at regional and rural shows. "This tastes like heaven."

He chuckled. "You always did love your food."

Her eyes flicked back open as something brushed the corner of her mouth. Bradley placed the napkin back on the table, but otherwise didn't move. "Sorry." He looked anything but sorry. "You had a little spot of cream and I couldn't resist."

His mouth was inches away from hers, and she stared at him with censure. "Bradley, we grew up together, went to the same school. Hung out together as friends."

"And that's the way you want it to stay," he muttered, looking more than a little deflated. "I get it."

She smiled and covered his hand with her own. "You know I'll always love you." *But only ever as a friend.*

"Scarlet."

She jerked back, pressing a hand to her mouth. Not just because her professional name sounded like a clap of thunder, and had been announced to all and sundry, but because the one man who'd been constantly in her thoughts had somehow found his way here.

She turned around. Mackenzie stood beside Mrs. Gracie, dwarfing the older lady. "What are you doing here?" she squeaked.

"I could ask the same of you." His stare was cutting. "Does your boyfriend know about me?"

Boyfriend. She gaped at him. Was he serious? Hurt twisted her belly, even as shame burned across her face. "I'm visiting an old friend," she said in a level voice, even as she wanted to scream and cry and stamp her feet.

His eyes glittered. "Do you tell all your friends you love them?" he gritted.

Mrs. Gracie sent Claire a considering look. "What's going on, Claire?"

Bradley stepped forward. "Is everything okay?"

She nodded, even as she pushed to her feet and glanced at Mrs. Gracie and back to Bradley. "I'm sorry to cut short my visit, but ... I've lost my appetite. I think I'll head home."

Bradley bristled, clearly suspecting the worst. He stood beside his grandmother. "Claire, if you need me, you know where I am."

She sent him a weak smile. "Thank you."

Mackenzie gave them a curt nod, and then put a hand on the small of her back to guide her through the house and out the front door. The moment they were clear, she turned to him and hissed, "How dare you show up here! This is my *personal life*. And you don't belong in it!"

She glimpsed fleeting pain, before his face became a mask and she wondered if she'd imagined it. He swept a hand toward the house. "And that man in there belongs in your personal life?"

"Yes, he does." She shook her head. "You don't always get what you want, Mackenzie. I'm not one of your many possessions. My free time is to do with what I want."

She spun on her heel, about to walk away, but he clapped a hand on her elbow and twisted her to face him. "Your time is hardly free. I paid for you this whole weekend, remember?" he growled. "If you want me to ring Maisey to confirm it, I'll be more than happy to."

"You wouldn't dare," she whispered, but she could see in his hard, uncompromising face, he'd do that and more.

"You know I would ... *Claire*."

She gasped, a whole kaleidoscope of emotions barreling through her at hearing him say her name. Despite it going against her work ethic she wanted to hear him say it again, wanted to pretend that being plain, ordinary Claire meant as much to him as sex goddess Scarlet did.

She bit her bottom lip, needing the pain to distract her from giving into him. "What do you want from me?"

"Damn it, Claire, isn't it obvious?" He blew out a hard breath, before tucking his hand around her elbow and escorting her to his car. A dark, low-slung sports model she'd never seen before.

It took no more than a minute or two at most before he pulled into her driveway.

Were there any more rules left to be broken? Her anonymity was to be protected at all costs, and yet she'd given it all away to a client who had drilled through the protective barriers of her heart with remarkable ease.

He killed the engine and turned to her. "Just give me what's left of this weekend, okay?"

She stared straight ahead, torn between longing for him and disgust that he was taking advantage of her profession to keep both the women he wanted in his life. "What about Emma?" she said woodenly, determined not to let envy creep into her voice.

"She's sound asleep." He exhaled heavily. "I just hope the second I'm out of her sight she doesn't go running back to the sack of shit she married."

She unclipped her seatbelt and climbed out of the car before he had a chance to open her door. She was paid to have sex with men, yet the thought of Mackenzie keeping a married woman in his bed while he fucked Claire on the side almost tied her heart in knots.

You're Scarlet now ... not Claire. Never Claire with Mackenzie.

He appeared at her side. "Look, I'll tell you everything you want to know about Emma tomorrow. I might even have my head wrapped around the whole thing by then. But the rest of today ... I want it to be just you and me."

Pain seared its way through her veins. This was why she should have stayed away from Mackenzie. She'd known from the start he had the power to hurt her, had recognized an undeniable attraction in their client–call girl relationship that trod on dangerous ground.

She lifted her chin. All she could do now was fall back on her role as his fantasy woman, dredge up every last ounce of her acting ability, knowing that after this weekend they were over.

He'd go back to Emma, while she'd go back to clients who wanted nothing more from her than her body.

In the meantime, there was one rule she would never break. "I won't conduct business in my own home."

His face tightened even as he nodded. "Of course not." He dug in his pocket for his phone. "I'll book a room for us tonight at the Sheraton."

She managed a smile. Any other call girl would be happy getting fucked in luxury. Despite her earlier warning, deep down she wanted only to take him into her modest home and spend the night with him in her bed, and pretend they were a normal couple.

She saw a curtain twitch in a window of the house next door. She sighed and opened her front door. She couldn't afford what the neighborhood gossip might do for her career. Do to her sisters.

Of course if Mrs. Gracie or Bradley put two and two together, idle gossip would be the least of her concerns.

She paused on the threshold, glancing up at his forbidding profile before she said tightly, "You might as well come in."

Chapter Nine

Mackenzie nodded. As far as invitations went, it left a lot to be desired. Yet his step was eager as he entered Scarlet's home.

No, not Scarlet. Claire. She'd always be Claire to him now.

The dining, lounge and kitchen were one open room, and spotlessly clean. A real home, the very opposite to the house he'd grown up in. But what caught his attention were the photos decorating the cream walls. A hutch revealed even more pictures, alongside decorative plates and vases.

"I'll freshen up, get changed and pack an overnight bag," Claire said, before pointing to a small bar opposite the cabinet. "Help yourself to a drink."

He nodded, and as she walked down a hallway and into her bedroom, he strode toward the photos on the wall. The biggest portrait revealed Claire with two younger, identical women and a pretty middle-aged woman.

He could see the resemblance in all of them. The dark-haired twins were drop-dead gorgeous, and he could only imagine the mischief and mayhem they'd put Claire through. It was also obvious their mother had been a beauty in her day, but even in the photo she looked faded and weary around the edges.

He guessed the shot had been taken not long after she'd been diagnosed. Sadness for Claire, for the whole family, plucked at his damn heartstrings. He scraped a hand over his face. He was getting too bloody sentimental. But nothing about his feelings for Claire were simple. He'd fallen for her hard; it'd just taken him eighteen months too long to realize he couldn't live without her.

He moved on to another photo, where Claire stared out to sea as she sat on a white-gold beach in a little yellow bikini. She was a sex goddess, and yet she didn't seem aware of it. He had a feeling she viewed her body as simply the key to a bank vault. Her call girl career was nothing more than a way to pay the bills and keep her sisters in comfort.

His stare narrowed. He had no doubt Claire had shouldered the brunt of financial and emotional stress for the twins.

He swung away from the photos and paced the small room. He'd do anything to take care of her. But hearing her tell another man she loved him still cut him up inside. It'd been a knife to his heart and a swift kick to his balls all at the same time. In that one moment he'd almost turned and walked away for good, let her be with the man she loved. But then his better judgment kicked in and shook off his momentary weakness.

He had the rest of the weekend to help her change her mind. To make her realize the other man wasn't the one she loved.

If only his weakness hadn't also transformed into seething rage that the one woman he wanted with everything he had, wanted someone else. If only it hadn't taken all his willpower not to act on the rage that had erupted inside him when he'd overheard Claire's admission.

As a businessman he relied on being cool, calm and composed. But the more he wanted Claire in his life, the more ready he was to tear any opposition apart with his bare hands.

His breath shuddered. What he wouldn't do to hear her say she loved him. To see her eyes shine with more than physical passion. He wanted her heartfelt adoration. But more than anything he wanted her trust, because without it she'd never be his, not in the way that truly mattered.

He sensed her presence a nanosecond before her faint tread had him pivoting to face her. "Wow."

She put down her overnight bag and smiled self-consciously at his approval. Her sexy, lilac dress plunged front and back, its cinched waist falling in gossamer layers to her knees. Even her high-heeled strappy shoes were sexy.

Her hair was piled up into its usual upsweep, but long wisps framed her face at the sides, and she tucked a strand behind her ear with a restless hand. Damn, she really was self-conscious. Somehow it made him want her all the more. She was a contradiction of fire and ice, sexuality and reservation.

His dick jerked and he suppressed a wry grin. He looked forward to taking her to the room he'd booked for the night, just the same as he looked forward to bringing her pleasure. Her little cries of ecstasy turned him on like nothing else. There had to be nothing better in the world than watching her fall apart beneath him.

He reached for her overnight bag, his dick twitching yet again. "Ready?" he asked huskily.

She looked surprised when a few minutes later he pulled up outside a local steakhouse. "We're eating first?" she asked.

He raised a brow. "I know how much you enjoy your food, the same as me." *Almost as much as we enjoy sex.* He grinned. "I'm sure we'll work off the calories and then some later tonight."

The restaurant was overflowing with patrons, but when the young waitress saw him approach, her eyes lit up with recognition. No doubt she'd read about him in the social or business pages of the latest newspaper.

It was one of the negatives of being a wealthy bachelor. Women found his wallet as attractive as his physicality. His lips thinned. His personality ... well, more often than not, it barely rated a mention in the grand scheme of things.

He'd hoped his single status would change sooner rather than later, had staked his life that although Claire slept with men for money, what frightened her most was her attraction to him as a whole. One that had little to do with the size of his bank balance.

Except now the game had changed, and he'd discovered his usually faultless instincts were totally skewed. She was in love with another man. Someone who didn't even appear to have money, and likely wasn't a client.

"Right this way," the waitress said, leading them to a small, intimate table at the end of the rectangular, bricked room.

Claire smiled up at him as he pulled out her seat before he took his own. He ordered a bottle of wine, and as the waitress departed he turned his attention back to Claire. The flame of a squat red candle flickered, chasing away the shadows and illuminating her face.

His chest ached with longing. She could have been a Madonna in a painting of old.

She cleared her throat and looked around. "I didn't even know about this place."

He nodded. "It's only been open for a few months. But there've been some great reviews."

She smiled at him like he was the keeper of knowledge. He resisted snorting. If he was so damn smart he would have done everything in his power to keep her eighteen months ago. Instead he'd let his pride and hurt feelings rule over his heart.

"Looks like I need to get out more." She lifted a hand. "At least in my own suburb. This place is a gem."

"Then let's hope it lives up to its reputation."

The waitress returned with their wine, uncorked and then poured it into two flutes. "Are you ready to order?" she asked.

Claire reached for her menu, skim-read it and said, "I'll have the rib fillet steak, medium-rare, the baked potato and a small side salad."

Mackenzie added, "I'll have the same, but medium-well with the steak."

Once the waitress took their menus and left them in peace, he reached over and clasped her hand. He had to ask her the one question that had been bothering him ever since he'd overheard her words to another man. Had to ask even if it half-killed him to hear it. "Claire," she visibly stiffened at hearing her real name, but he continued undaunted, "do you really have feelings for that man you were with earlier?"

"Bradley?"

He nodded. "I'm guessing that's him. You said you loved him."

She stared up at him, as though seeing him for the first time. "Why do you even care?"

"Why do you find it so hard to believe that I do?"

She blinked up at him, emotions flicking across her face so fast he couldn't pin one down to define just exactly what she was feeling. "You pay to be with me. Why would you even want more from me than that?"

He frowned. "Do you think you're not worthy of anything more meaningful than sex with a man?"

Damn it. They were getting nowhere, one question following another, following another.

She withdrew her hand from his clasp, and he felt her distance like a physical blow. She drank some of her wine, placed the glass down carefully and said, "It's my job to believe exactly that."

"Then how do you feel about me? *Really* feel?" he asked. God, he needed to hear the truth like he needed air. What she said next could change everything between them.

She blinked again, but this time it looked like she was driving back tears when she asked, "More to the point, how do you feel about Emma?"

"Emma?" It took too many seconds for realization to set in. *Holy shit*. She really thought he was that low? It might have been funny if the situation wasn't so damn serious. "I love Emma, of course I do. But not in the way you think."

~

Claire swallowed back jealousy as she took another mouthful of her wine. She didn't want to know about his feelings for Emma, and yet she needed to hear it.

"So you love her, but you're not *in* love with her?" she asked.

He nodded. "Yes, that's it exactly."

Her belly lurched. "Does Emma know?"

He smiled, his face tender. "Of course she does. She's my sister."

She gaped at him, jealousy, envy and a whole shitload of unwanted emotions draining out of her. "Seriously?"

His hand covered hers. "Yes, seriously. I'm sorry if you were misled into thinking otherwise." His thumb stroked her knuckles. "Guess I should have had some photos on the walls of my cabin after all. Then you would have seen the resemblance and known right away I had a sister."

She blew out an unsteady breath. "I just wish you'd told me sooner."

"I wish you'd asked me sooner. Just as I wish you never thought I'd stoop so low as to have a woman in my bed at home while sleeping with you in a hotel room."

She blinked. He was right. He was an honorable man, despite the cutthroat world he lived in. Though she had no doubt he'd do anything for the woman he loved.

Their food arrived then, and Claire inhaled the aromas with renewed enthusiasm, her belly sharp with hunger.

Mackenzie thanked the waitress, who seemed overly eager to please, before he smiled at Claire and said, "Let's eat."

Claire couldn't remember a meal that tasted half as good. It was as if all her positive energy had made her appreciate every bite. Happiness danced across her tastebuds and re-energized her, warmth stealing through her veins and settling between her thighs.

God, she couldn't wait to get to his room and make love to him. Even her nipples felt sensitized, eager for Mackenzie to pull each one into his mouth, and lick and suck ...

The waitress led a group of young men to an empty table behind them. Claire glanced at them and gaped at seeing Bradley in the group. But of course if this place had just opened and already buzzed with reputation, many of the locals would be dining here.

Bradley stared back at her and her smile faded. Something felt ... off. He wasn't the same laid-back man she'd seen hours before. Wasn't the same easygoing, friendly guy she'd grown up with. He looked keyed-up and on edge.

She looked away, hiding her frown. She only hoped Mrs. Gracie was okay. But surely Bradley would drop by her table and let her know if something was wrong.

Mackenzie leaned forward and murmured, "So ... are you going to tell me now your feelings for the man behind you?"

She leaned forward, their heads almost touching. The last thing she wanted was for Bradley to overhear their conversation, though the muted roar of conversation going on around them would surely drown out their voices. "I told him I loved him ... but he knew it was only as a friend."

Mackenzie's gaze sharpened. "He wanted more?"

She nodded. "Yes. But I don't feel that way about him."

"What about me?" His eyes glinted, before a half-smile pulled at his lips. "On second thought, don't tell me. Not here. I want you to tell me in complete privacy."

He leaned forward a little more then, his lips brushing across hers. A tender kiss that underscored possessiveness she couldn't deny. He pulled back, his gaze snaring hers. "I vote for bypassing dessert."

She nodded. "I do too."

Cake or pie didn't compare to the multiple orgasms he'd give her. Didn't compare at all.

They both stood, and Mackenzie clasped her hand even as she froze on hearing snatches of conversation.

"A whore? No. Way."

"Wish I could afford to fuck her."

"Nothing that damn sexy is free."

"Man I'd do anything for a piece of that pussy—"

Claire withheld a gasp and pressed a fist to her churning belly. If Mackenzie heard the conversation, he gave no indication other than a tightening of his jaw. His hand squeezed hers before he led her out of the dining room and toward the front of the restaurant where he paid and generously tipped. A minute later he guided her toward his car and opened the passenger door.

She looked ahead, unable to think or feel. Hurt was a poisonous barb deep inside her heart. Bradley had been her childhood friend; one she'd thought would always have her back.

She couldn't have been more wrong.

Chapter Ten

Mackenzie drove through the congested Sydney traffic, withholding a fury that had almost disabled him the moment he'd overheard the sickening conversation about Claire.

But as much as he'd wanted to knock some heads together over such blatant disrespect, he'd refused to give in to the violent urges that his father had fallen victim to. He refused to follow in the footsteps of the one parent he loathed. A pity it'd almost killed him to stay silent and strong.

Whatever Bradley had been to Claire, it was over now. But what burned Mackenzie the most was that *he* was likely the one responsible for Bradley's changed perception.

Little wonder she hid her profession and became the mysterious Scarlet.

He glanced Claire's way. Despite the brave front, she looked too damn fragile. The intimate, happy mood from earlier had faded away like it'd never been.

He blew out a steadying breath. There was only one thing for it. He'd make love to her tonight and make her forget everything but pleasure. His jaw clenched. His instincts urged him to protect her, to take her away from the very profession that both sustained and slowly destroyed her. Except if it hadn't been for her profession, he'd probably never have met her, never have fallen for the woman behind the gorgeous exterior.

He pulled up at the hotel and a porter retrieved their luggage while a valet parked the car. Mackenzie took care of their booking at the reception desk, before he placed a hand on the small of Claire's back and guided her toward the bank of elevators.

Not even a minute later they stepped into the luxurious suite, where floor to ceiling windows showcased panoramic views of Darling Harbour. He flicked on the lights. He doubted Claire noticed much of anything. He'd soon change that. Closing the door with a snap, he said huskily, "Come here."

She turned, releasing a shuddering sigh before she stepped into his arms like she needed to be there. Her lips were soft and responsive under his, and he groaned against her mouth as he cupped her ass, loving the gentle curve of her cheeks, the press of her generous breasts against his chest.

God, even her scent drove him wild. Apple blossom and the ocean, fresh and clean, yet sexy and wild. A contradiction that was perfectly her.

He drove his tongue into her mouth, tasting her, exploring her, even as he propelled her backwards until she fell onto the bed. He followed her down, kissing her deep, drinking in the little moans that thrummed a nerve straight to his cock.

He pulled away only long enough to drag the dress over her head. A tearing sound filled the air, and Claire stared up at him, "It has little buttons at the side."

He grinned, passion and heat pulsing through him like an addiction as he threw the torn dress aside, a button glinting as it arced through the air. He didn't much care. Not while she lay beneath him like a siren, the generous handful of her breasts bared to him and her nipples puckering under his gaze. He wanted her completely naked, yet somehow her cream thong showcased her gorgeous body to perfection. "I'll buy you a dozen more of the same dress."

He kissed her again, taking control of her mouth, her body. Pushing his fingers through her hair and taking her inexorably toward that special place she needed to be.

A knock on the door followed by an announcement of their luggage had him reluctantly pull away. "Don't move," he commanded hoarsely, before he pulled the door open a crack and thrust the porter a tip from his wallet.

Dumping the bags inside, he snapped the door shut once again and prowled toward her. God, she was beautiful. She could be a Victoria's Secret model in a sexy, underwear photo shoot—minus the bra. Except she was ten times hotter and far more fascinating. Not to mention totally aroused.

He stilled at the edge of the bed and looked down at her. Heaven help him, he didn't just want to get inside her body, he wanted to get inside her head and uncover everything.

She blinked and smiled up at him with her passion-plump lips. His dick strained behind his jeans even before he bent and slid her thong to one side, exposing her gorgeous pussy. He touched the sensitive flesh inside her labia, and she jerked against his hand, needing so much more.

He swallowed. Hard. His willpower was already worn to a thread, and he didn't want to think about it snapping anytime soon. He was too lost in the moment. Too busy watching her expression and drinking in her every emotion.

She writhed under him as his forefinger circled a path around her sensitive spot. He didn't touch her clit; he wanted her panting and insane with need first, wanted a climax to grab her by the throat with its intensity, and be so all-consuming that nothing penetrated her utter bliss.

"I need you inside me," she whimpered. "I need you *now*."

Holy shit. His willpower frayed to the point of no return as she pulled off her thong and unclipped her bra. He swore softly, before he unzipped his jeans to release his dick.

Her eyes widened at seeing him commando once again. He shook his head. "You should know by now I never wear anything under my jeans," he rasped, before he pulled her to the edge of the bed. He stepped between her thighs. She wrapped her legs around his hips, her pretty pink cunt shining with need.

He didn't need to ask her if she was ready for him, she was dripping wet and as desperate as he was for him to sink deep into her heat. He thrust into her, filling her, stretching her inner flesh, which molded around his shaft.

He groaned. Nothing could possibly feel this fucking good. He retreated and then plunged deep, taking up a rhythm that had her tits bouncing in time to his strokes and her moans increasing in volume. His balls tightened. Shit. He wasn't going to last. He thumbed her clit and pushed her straight into climax.

She shrieked as she came, and he poured himself into her with a satisfied groan, his heart and soul singing with pleasure.

Claire smiled up at Mackenzie, aware things really had changed between them. Whatever barriers she'd erected no longer seemed necessary. She had nothing to hide from him, had nothing to fear. He was everything and so much more than she wanted in a man.

Not only was he amazing in bed and gave her mind-blowing orgasms, he was sensitive to her needs. Oh, he was tough and uncompromising—he wouldn't have gone so far professionally if he wasn't—but on a personal level he'd given all of himself to her, put his heart on the line to show her exactly how much he loved her.

Her legs fell from his like loose spaghetti as he disengaged. She sighed happily. It really was time she returned the favor and told him her true feelings. "Mack," she whispered, her heart beating double-time. "There's something I need to tell you."

"Yes?"

Her smile faded at his one-worded emotional retreat, her chest aching for the man who believed she was breaking bad news. "I love you."

He froze, his features settling into shock, before softening with adoration. "I love you too." He shook his head, his lips curling with delight. "I'd despaired that I'd never hear you say those words."

Her heart swelled and her vision misted. "I never thought I'd say those words either," she said softly. Hell, she never thought in a million years she'd get her own happily ever after.

He bent, kissing her softly, before he lifted her against his chest and carried her effortlessly into a spacious bathroom. "A shower first," he said huskily, "then we'll talk about this some more."

Half an hour later, thoroughly soaped and clean thanks to Mackenzie's tender ministrations, she stood outside with him on their suite's wraparound patio. The night was velvet soft, with thousands of lights sparkling like diamonds in the darkness.

He sighed softly, and she looked up at him and asked, "What's wrong?"

He turned to her and even in the shadows she could see the gleam in his eyes. He lifted a hand and touched one side of her face. She leaned into him, so content it was almost a crime.

"Claire, I've never been happier."

"Me neither," she admitted softly.

He stepped behind her, his arms going around her waist and his chin resting on her scalp. "All those lights out there, all those people, and yet I somehow find my soulmate."

She closed her eyes, her acceptance of him complete. Mackenzie had always been the one man for her, she'd just been too busy fighting her feelings, too scared to admit that maybe he was the one man in her life who wouldn't walk away. Wouldn't abandon her for someone else.

"I really do love you," she said, needing to tell him again. Needing him to hear it.

His clasp tightened, powerful feelings rolling off him in waves and shrouding her with love. “I know you do,” he said huskily. “And just so you know ... you’re the love of my life. The only woman I’ve ever wanted now and in the future.”

She put her hands over his. He mightn’t have proposed marriage, but it was close to the real thing. He was committing to her, letting her know he’d be faithful to her.

She’d be a fool to imagine he wouldn’t expect the same in return. She turned in his arms and looked up at him. “I don’t want to be with anyone else either.” One of his hands moved to gently massage her bared back, thanks to her low-cut negligee. “I’m ready to leave my profession and be with you.”

If she was being honest, she’d been ready to leave for months ... ever since Mackenzie had bought a night of her time. He’d turned her world upside down, made her yearn for things she’d thought were out of her reach.

“You really mean that?” he asked, the uncertainty that almost broke his voice close to breaking her heart.

“More than anything.”

His thumb traced her soft skin. “Let’s go to bed,” he said silkily, “I need to hold you tight, and never let you go again.”

Chapter Eleven

Claire had a bounce in her step the next morning as she walked up to her front door with Mackenzie by her side, his hand engulfing hers. She no longer cared who saw them together. She wasn't going to hide her feelings anymore—unlike Mackenzie who'd been open and upfront with his affections from the very start.

If only she hadn't gotten scared knowing how easily she could fall for him, then maybe she wouldn't have lied and told him she didn't return his feelings. Then maybe she could have been this happy eighteen months ago.

The sun warmed her scalp as she unlocked her front door before he turned her around to face him. He bent and kissed her with a lingering tenderness that left her aching for more. He smiled when he finally pulled free. "See you soon, Claire."

Her heart almost burst with love. She would never get enough of hearing him say her name. Her real name. She reached up, and blotted a smear of lipstick from his mouth with her thumb. "Say hello to your sister for me."

He nodded. "When she's herself again, I'd really love you two to meet."

Claire smiled. Could a man be any more amazing? A caring family man and an attentive lover all rolled into one. "I'd love that." She cocked her head to the side. "Is it selfish of me to tell you to hurry back?"

He grinned. "Unless my sister is an emotional wreck, I don't plan on staying too long."

He bent his head and gave her one last kiss, before turning to stride back to his car. She waved as the engine growled into life, and then she stood and watched as he drove down her street and out of sight.

She touched her still tingling lips, aware her body and soul were awash with elation. She was totally, unequivocally in love with Mackenzie, and knew he felt the same in return. She only wished she'd trusted that things would work out from the very start. Trusted that she deserved to be loved and adored by someone like Mackenzie.

Her neighbor's curtain twitched once again, and Claire lifted her hand once more to give her neighbor a jaunty wave. With an ear-splitting grin, she turned and walked inside.

Ten minutes later, her overnight bag unpacked and her excitement ceding to weariness, she ran a bath. Adding a splash of fragrant vanilla bath oil, she slid into the tub's deep warmth with a ragged sigh.

She closed her eyes. How fortunate was she to have not only met Mackenzie, but have someone like him want her permanently in his life? She'd never expected to fall in love with him—with anyone—let alone fully trust a man. She'd instead allowed herself to believe all men were like her father. That all men imagined the grass was greener elsewhere.

Her lips twitched. It was safe to say she was happier and more relaxed now than she'd been in a very long time. Of course she still had to ring Maisey and tell her the news. The madam wouldn't be happy, but then no-one in the sex industry lasted long term. Youth and good looks faded, even as the women became jaded and weary of the game.

But Maisey knew as well as anyone that Claire—Scarlet—was way too young to retire from the business. It wouldn't go down well with the madam to lose yet another prime worker to a client.

Claire sank fully under the water, drowning out any bit of guilt. She didn't owe Maisey anything. The madam had made more than enough money from her. Mackenzie had seen to that.

Her lungs were screaming for air by the time she resurfaced to a sharp rap on her front door. She sucked in a breath and climbed out of the tub with a silly grin on her face and butterflies dancing in her belly. When Mack had said he wouldn't be long, she'd thought he'd meant at least a couple of hours!

She knotted a fluffy white towel around her and raced down the hallway. She threw open the door. "I wasn't expecting you this—" She froze, eyes widening. *Shit.* "Bradley ... what are you doing here?" she squeaked.

He looked her slowly up and down. "You were expecting another man?"

It was a barbed comment, his accusation clear. Not that he tried to hide his scorn. "You didn't think I wouldn't uncover just exactly what you are now, *Scarlet*?" He said her name like he'd fished it out of a sewer. "I looked up all the call agencies and found the VIP Desire Agency. One of their escorts called Scarlet perfectly matched your description."

She gasped, moving to slam the door shut, but he put out an arm and easily kept it open. "I won't be ignored this time, Scarlet." He moved inside, shutting the front door behind him with one hand and clasping her upper arm with the other. "I only want what you give out to other men."

She stared up at him, her hair dripping, her throat dry and her belly twisting with both dread and denial. "This isn't you, Bradley. I know you better than—"

"Shut up!" he roared, as though all his pent-up emotions were released in the flick of a switch. He was no longer the boy she used to know, not even close.

She didn't see his backhand coming until it was too late. She dropped to the floor, pain lighting through her cheekbone and humiliation searing deep into her soul. She looked up, but there was no kindness in the man she'd thought she knew. Bradley was a stranger, whose lust burned like a cold flame in his stare.

"Don't do this, Bradley," she whispered.

She'd had a couple of frightening experiences in the past with other men, but she'd never known this kind of cold violence from a man who'd always treated her with respect and kindness.

His eyes flashed. "Take off your towel."

She pushed to her feet, and lifted her chin. "No." She wouldn't be intimidated, wouldn't let her one-time friend imagine she was wicked and immoral when he was guilty of far worse.

"What did you say?" Bradley snarled.

Her chin tilted higher. "I said no. I won't go naked in front of you."

He stepped forward, his eyes flashing raw fury and lust. "You want my money, is that it?" He dragged his wallet out of his back pocket and threw a bill her way. "Consider me a client."

She shook her head, feeling sorry for the man she thought had everything. But maybe growing up with his loving grandmother hadn't been enough for him. Maybe underneath all his charm had been a resentful little boy with deep emotional issues. She pointed to the front door. "Get out, Bradley."

Indecision for a moment held him still, but then he closed the distance between them in one step. It took him one more second to wrench off her towel before he clamped his mouth over hers in a brutal kiss that was all about his own needs.

She tried to pull away, but he splayed one hand behind her nape while his other mauled her breast, pinching and squeezing her nipple. She cried out, but he only mashed his lips harder against hers, making it impossible to breathe, to even think.

But she wasn't some impotent female; she'd watched her mother die, had brought up her sisters, and had dealt with men far meaner than

Bradley. She opened her mouth and, as he shoved his tongue inside, she bit down hard.

The coppery tang of blood filled her mouth even as he jerked away from her with a roar. He wiped the back of his mouth with his hand, smearing blood. He grinned maniacally. "I was going to make it good for you too, but I guess you like it rough."

She stepped back and he followed, his eyes glittering as he drank in her nudity. He unzipped his jeans, the rasp magnified in the thick silence of the room. Her breath hitched, coldness pinching her insides. She might sleep with men for money, but it'd always been on her own terms, with men who'd stayed strangers ... until Mackenzie.

She spun on her heel and ran, but got no further than three or four steps before Bradley caught her and dragged her around to face him, his grip crushing her forearm.

"Don't go now, Scarlet, the fun has only started."

He slammed her against the wall and pinned her there with more strength than she'd imagined he possessed. But he didn't kiss her this time, instead he sucked and then bit her shoulder, his fingers digging into her breasts, groping and squeezing.

She closed her eyes against his assault, against the reality of her friend committing such an offense. "Stop, Bradley. Stop it now!"

When the pressure eased the smallest amount, she knew it was now or never to catch him by surprise, and knee him hard in the groin. But suddenly his weight left her. She opened her eyes to Mackenzie throwing Bradley against the opposite wall. Plaster crumbled and Bradley's face paled at his opposition's strength and obvious rage.

Bradley put his hands up in supplication. "Easy, man. I thought you were her client, that's all. Easy mistake to make."

Mackenzie's expression hardened and he lifted his fist and drove it into Bradley's face. "Shut your damn mouth." Blood gushed from Bradley's nose, and he whimpered in pain and fear. A vein in Mackenzie's jaw throbbed even as he grabbed a handful of Bradley's shirt and lifted him high. "You go near my woman again, and I will not be responsible for my actions."

Bradley nodded. "Of course." He turned panicked eyes Claire's way. "I'm sorry. I never meant to hurt you."

Her vision blurred, a hot tear rolling down her cheek. She retrieved her towel and wrapped her body from Bradley's eyes. "Yes, you did, you bastard," she choked out. He'd uncovered what she did for a living and he'd hated her for it. Hated that she'd slept with strangers and never once slept with him.

He'd wanted to hurt her as much as he imagined she'd hurt him.

Despite his obvious lack of air flow, Bradley's face reddened as much from foolish rage. "You knew how I felt! I could have had anyone but I only ever wanted you! And then I come home to find out you're a goddamned whore!"

Mackenzie threw Bradley across the room. She gaped. She'd never seen such power, such raw violence. Mackenzie was the epitome of control, but going by his clenched fists, his flared nostrils and rigid shoulders, right then nothing reined him back. He looked ready to pulverize the other man.

Bradley rolled, and then scrambled to his feet. But it was the look of abject fear on his face as Mackenzie stalked toward him that sent Claire running to stop any more violence.

Mackenzie lifted a fist and she stood between it and Bradley. "Mack, don't," she said quietly, searching his face, his hard and uncompromising stare, until a flicker of something close to calm signaled he hadn't tipped right over the edge. Yet.

She barely noticed Bradley staggering for the front door. Barely heard his retreating footsteps as he made a quick getaway. Instead all her attention stayed on Mackenzie, waiting as his bleak rage settled into something close to composure.

He lifted an unsteady hand, touching her swollen cheek, the top of her bruised breast and the imprinted teeth marks on her shoulder. "I'll send for my doctor," he said hoarsely.

She shook her head and drew in a shuddering breath. "There's no need. I'm fine. But what about you? Are you okay? You looked like you lost it for a minute."

Mackenzie peered at his knuckles, which were smeared with Bradley's blood. His face blanched, his eyes going dark before he dropped his arm and looked away. Holy shit, he acted as though the sins were all his.

"I'm sorry, Claire," he said brokenly. "It seems I'm like my father after all."

You're nothing like your father! Except no words made it past the ever-growing lump in her throat.

He shook his head, and echoed, "I'm so very sorry."

He turned and walked to the front door. Panic filled her, more even than when Bradley had attacked her. The reality of loving a woman like her was clearly hitting him hard. She swallowed, and said hoarsely, "That sounds like goodbye."

Mackenzie stopped, and then half turned. He nodded. "You're better off without me."

She stared, trying hard not to let her emotions spill free, when all she wanted was to sob and beg him to stay. Never leave her. "I think what you're trying to say is that *you* are better off without me," she said softly.

He shook his head, his voice cracking. "You know that's not true."

"Maybe Bradley *is* right. I'm a whore. No decent man would want me, knowing that."

He spun and faced her fully, before he strode back to her. "Don't ever let anyone make you think that. There's not a man on the planet who wouldn't wish you were his."

"And yet you're leaving," she said quietly, even as her heart was breaking into a hundred little pieces. She wouldn't beg. Not for anything. Her mother had begged and Claire had seen her father's disgust and rejection as clearly as she'd seen his desperation to leave all the quicker.

Mackenzie glanced down at his bloodied hands. "You'll thank me one day." He stared at her one last time, as though imprinting her on his mind. Then he swung away and stalked out of her opened front door, with not even a last, backward glance.

It was only when she heard the distant sound of his engine start up that she sank to her knees and let her tears fall free.

Chapter Twelve

Mackenzie sat in his office chair brooding about everything but the task at hand. His business, the one thing that had been his mainstay in life, couldn't now hold his attention.

It'd been ten days since he'd walked out on Claire. He flicked a glance at his gold Cartier watch. Ten days and seven hours to be more precise. And he'd never been more miserable or discontent.

Not when those ten days had been spent imagining her with other clients. Ten days of mentally hearing her little gasps as someone else pleasured her, or worse, as she pleasured them. Even imagining her smiling at another man, her sexy little laugh reserved for the client paying for her time, ate him up inside.

But he'd stayed away from her because he feared he no longer had control of his seesawing emotions, and that maybe he had inherited the explosive temper gene from his father after all.

But it was proving an impossible task when he also had to be a mental rock for his sister while she went through her grieving crisis. Lord help him, all he'd wanted was to share in her tears. The pain in his chest was growing worse each day, not dulling to the ache he'd hoped.

His hands fisted. Better grief than anger. The last thing he wanted or needed was another fit of jealousy to boil over into rage.

He swore, swiping at the neatly stacked reams of paperwork and getting minimal satisfaction in watching them fan into the air, before they scattered in a mess across the floor. Fuck. He needed to get the hell out of here. Go for a run. Have a strong drink. Anything but sit numbly in his office.

He had enough execs who'd do cartwheels over the added responsibility of running his varied businesses. Regan and Terry were young go-getters. In fact, it might prove interesting to see how they handled the challenge.

He blew out a heavy breath and pushed out of his chair to stand at the huge windows overlooking the harbor. Late afternoon sunlight glinted on a dozen yachts lazily sailing through the turquoise waters, a pristine picture that, right then, irritated the hell out of him.

What was the point of money and prestige, not to mention power, if inside he was desolate? Not even his sister's slow return to physical and mental good health could distract him from all-consuming thoughts of Claire. Without her in his life, everything had become colorless and grey.

But if being without her was his biggest worry, then unstoppable fury was a close second. He'd witnessed his father's violence, and never wanted to emulate him in any way. Yet savagery had erupted inside him at seeing Bradley hurting Claire, an unquenchable urge to ensure the motherfucker never hurt her ever again.

A tap on the door snapped his train of thought, and he swung around to face his middle-aged secretary with a growled. "What now, Matilda?" He dragged a hand over his face and said, "Bloody hell. Tell me I haven't been a complete and utter bastard these last few days."

"You *have* been a complete and utter bastard, sir," Matilda said blandly. "But it's nice to know you're human."

His chuckle held no warmth. "Does everyone imagine I'm not?"

"I believe most of us see you as a machine without any mortal weakness." She smiled. "It will reassure your staff to know you're not infallible ... sir."

"Well, thank you for your insight, Matilda. Your honesty is, as always, refreshing." He blew out a slow breath. "So, what is on my agenda for today?" He'd barely glanced at his schedule the last few days.

"You have an appointment with the head chef from Canterberry 89. He's waiting for you now."

Mackenzie nodded, recalling the talented chef who wanted to move the menu of the restaurant in a whole new direction. "Send him in." As she turned to do as he asked, he added, "And send Regan and Terry to me right after." He grinned, suddenly energized. "Their workload is about to get serious."

She arched a knowing brow. "As you wish."

His secretary was again about to leave when he called out, "One last thing." She turned back, and he said, "My apologies for everything I've put you through these last few days."

If he'd learned nothing else from his relationship with Claire, it was just how easily a man could trample over a woman's self-esteem.

Matilda's brow arched even higher. "You really have fallen hard ... sir."

As his secretary walked out the door, his chuckle this time was almost amused when he murmured to himself, "Yes, I most certainly have."

He stepped back toward his desk. Picking up his platinum pen, he rolled it through his fingers. He'd never been a violent man, had instinctively fought even the slightest compulsion. Surely all those even-tempered years had to count for something. He'd never in a million years hit a woman, and he sure as shit wouldn't hit a woman he loved.

The pen dug into his palm. He'd been a damn fool letting his father's failures become his own. For letting his father's sins dictate his own life. If he was lucky he hadn't left it too late to make amends with Claire. Because, although rejection was exactly what he deserved, he couldn't face one more night—one more minute—without her by his side.

He was totally, irrevocably in love with Claire. And he realized now that such a powerful emotion would keep even a hint of darkness at bay.

He glanced at his watch once again. His meetings would be concluded in record time.

~

Claire took one last look around the spotlessly clean house. It'd been ten days since she'd quit the VIP Desire Agency. Ten days alone to quietly grieve for the man she'd loved and lost, while deciding where her life was headed.

Her vision blurred and she blinked back the tears she'd been holding in. She wouldn't cry now! She was strong, smart, and more than capable of living without a man in her life. *Any* man in her life. She just had to reprogram herself to envision such a future.

She'd known the moment Mackenzie had walked out her front door that she couldn't return to work as a call girl. Her heart was no longer in it. Mackenzie was the one and only man she'd ever want. In her bed and out.

Cleaning her house and putting it on the market had been her next step toward her new life. It was time to move on. Start a new life. A new beginning. Maybe even find some small measure of happiness.

Now she just had to break the news to her sisters.

The doorbell chimed. She frowned. Danni and Tina should still be at their lectures. In fact, it'd be another half-an-hour at least before they arrived.

She dropped her dusty cleaning rag into the bin and headed to the front entrance. She peered through the thin strip of glazed glass on the side before she opened the door to a delivery man.

"Claire Davis?" the whiskered delivery man asked in a cheery voice.

She nodded. "Yes. That's me."

"This is for you." Claire signed a delivery slip before he handed her a long, elegant white box that was surprisingly heavy. Thanking him, she carried the box inside and put it on the table, before untying the huge ribbon holding the lid in place.

She swallowed past the lump in her throat as she pulled out a dozen dresses. They were the exact same style as the one Mackenzie had torn off her in a fit of lust, and had promised to replace. But only one of them was lilac colored. White, black, crimson, peach, canary-yellow and burnt orange were just some of the colors he'd ordered.

But it wasn't until she held up a rainbow-colored gown that emotions fizzed and sparked inside her. God she missed him. Missed his tender smile, his skilled touch and passionate kiss. His husky voice and his big body. His generosity and—

She mentally shook away the thoughts, even as she riffled through the dresses. There was no note, nothing to tell her if this extravagant gift was his way of saying goodbye, or even if it was his way of asking for forgiveness. She dropped the dresses back into the box, deliberately hardening her heart.

Mackenzie walking away from her had made her take a good, long look at her life. She refused to be her mother all over again. She'd handed Mackenzie her heart and he'd trampled all over it on his way to the door and out of her life. All she wanted now was to go someplace to heal, and gain some perspective on her future.

Bradley—and probably half the neighborhood—learning about her profession was just an added incentive to get away and start all over again. She only hoped and prayed the gossip hadn't reached her sisters' ears ... never reached them.

She was still mulling over things when she heard her sisters' sedan pull into the driveway, right on time. She smiled from the doorway as Tina and Danni climbed out of their shiny car and clattered on their heels toward her, dark hair flying and laughs filling the air.

Tina was the first to air her concern the moment they were inside and Claire told them her plans.

"Wow. What brought on this sudden decision?"

Claire shrugged. "I just feel like it's time for a change. Especially now that you girls can take care of yourselves."

Danni grimaced. "We know how much you've sacrificed for us since Mom died. And honestly, I think you're making the right decision." She swung out a hand. "Much as we all love this place, it's time to let another family make their memories here."

Claire smiled, feeling a little choked up. "Thanks, Danni." She looked around. "I can't believe this is the last time we'll all be together in this house before it goes up for auction tomorrow."

Tina sighed. "I think Mom would understand, be happy even, that we're moving on."

Claire hugged her sisters, trying not to cry and blubber like she was the younger sister, instead of the mature, older sister who was supposed to hold it together. She pulled back. "And just so you know the proceeds of the house will be split evenly between you both."

Tina frowned, her dark eyes assessing. "You paid for the house on your own, why would you give it all to us?"

Claire managed another smile that felt all too wobbly. "I have enough saved to keep me going for a while. And I want the financial security this house will give you girls. I'm sure Mom would want that too."

"But where will you go?" asked Danni. "What about your work?"

"I've told my boss I'm leaving. She understands."

That wasn't exactly the truth. Maisey had been livid, but had still managed to stay politely professional. The madam had even wished her well in her future endeavors.

Claire lifted a brow. "As for where I'm going ... I'm thinking I might start with an island hop around the Great Barrier Reef. Enjoy a bit of snorkelling, sip some margaritas. Chill out for a few weeks."

"Have sex with a few random guys?" Danni prompted.

Claire smiled. If only her sisters knew! Sex was the very last thing she'd be having. In fact, it felt kind of liberating knowing it wasn't even on the agenda. Not when sex with anyone but Mackenzie would feel stale and all kinds of wrong. But Danni and Tina didn't need to know that. "Who knows, maybe I will," she said vaguely.

"Claire ... what's going on? Are you leaving?"

She turned with a gasp at the one voice she never thought she'd hear again. But the man standing in the open doorway wasn't an apparition. "*Mack* ... what are you doing here?"

"I had to see you," he said starkly, his face tight and his eyes glinting.

She blinked, yearning stretching like a fragile bubble within. She shook her head, anger overriding all else. He couldn't just waltz back into her life! She was leaving. She'd already made up her mind. There was no room in her life for Mackenzie. For any man. She refused to get hurt again.

"Claire, is *he* the reason you're leaving?" Danni asked.

Mackenzie's eyes narrowed, his attention staying on Claire. "Please tell me that's not true," he said quietly. When she didn't immediately answer, he dragged his stare from her and stepped inside toward her sisters. "Hi, Tina, is it?" he asked, voice warm and his hand encompassing Danni's.

"No. Actually, I'm Danni," she said, thawing just a little as she looked Mackenzie up and down, and evidently finding nothing but positives.

"Nice to finally meet you," he murmured, before turning to the other twin. "And you too, Tina," he greeted.

Tina visibly melted. "Likewise. And don't worry, everyone gets us mixed up. You'll probably forget who is who the next time you see us."

Claire stood silent as Mackenzie and her sisters chatted. And despite herself, she feasted her eyes on the man constantly in her thoughts. He wore a suit like no-one else, like he was born and bred for designer clothes even as his whole demeanor screamed he'd been raised on the wrong side of the tracks.

"So how long have you two known each other?" Tina asked him.

"And where did you meet?" Danni added, her question somehow loaded with innuendo.

Mackenzie turned to Claire, and her every cell froze at his perceptive look. He knew not to tell her sisters anything about her profession—didn't he?

He turned back to the twins. "I first met Claire over eighteen months ago." His smile revealed a passion and warmth that couldn't be feigned. "I remember it like it was only yesterday. There was instant connection and chemistry—"

Claire cleared her throat. "Mack, I really don't think—"

"Don't stop now!" Danni and Tina interrupted at exactly the same time, before turning to one another with a conspiratorial giggle.

Mackenzie slid Claire another look, as if letting her know her secret was safe. Tension leached out of her just a little as he said, "It was a sweltering hot afternoon, with a storm forecast for later that night. I'd left work early to enjoy a cold beer at the bar a block from my office."

Claire didn't want to think about the day Scarlet had been ready to meet her new client. A pity Mackenzie's words sent her straight back in time. To the shivers of sensation of first making eye contact with him. The fluttering of excitement deep in her belly, her womb, at knowing she'd soon be underneath such a powerful, superb man.

Mackenzie paused a beat, as though savoring the memory right along with her. "Claire wore the most beautiful dress, sexy and seductive but elegant all at the same time. It was emerald green, her hair like a flame in contrast." He smiled. "All I could think about was taking her in my arms and pushing my fingers through her hair."

She swallowed. He'd done that and a whole lot more. He'd taken her to his hotel room and given her so much pleasure. She'd had one orgasm after another, until she'd been too weak to move, and too sated to care.

"Wow." Tina sent Claire an approving look. "Why haven't we heard about this man before now?"

Danni nodded and said drily, "Apparently she doesn't have time to date men."

Claire swallowed. Tina was by far the more romantic of the twins, she gushed over all things lovey-dovey while Danni preferred the cold hard facts. It was Danni she'd have to convince. Danni whose eyebrows pinched in the middle while Tina beamed at them both.

Claire cleared her throat. "I wasn't sure exactly where our ... relationship was going."

Mackenzie turned to her. "Weren't you?" He stepped toward her. "What if I said I've regretted leaving you every minute since walking out the door? What if I said I can't live without you in my life for another minute?" His voice softened. "What if I asked you to stay?"

She frowned, biting her bottom lip and only half-aware of her sisters' wide-eyed stares watching her every reaction. "Please don't," she whispered, focused on the man who already had too much power over her.

He'd break her if she let him. Crush what was left of her heart and destroy her soul in the process. No. She had to protect herself, had to cut the binds that tied her to him. Leave him before he had the opportunity in the future to leave her. "I'm going, Mack. And nothing's going to change my mind."

His eyes darkened as he took the final step to close the gap between them. His hands clasped hers. "What if I told you I really do love you?"

Her heart missed a beat even as she slowly shook her head. "Don't do this. Not now. You walked out on me. You don't get to have the final say."

His hands tightened and he closed his eyes for a second, shuttering his thoughts. Then he nodded and released her hands, taking a step back. "I can't force you to love me again. But I can't let you go ... not like this."

Her chest squeezed at his heartfelt words. She sucked in a steadying breath. She wouldn't give in, wouldn't allow herself to be blinded to reality. Even if he never again walked out on her, he'd always see her as a call girl.

And trust was a two-way street.

She lifted her chin. Starting again meant leaving this old life behind, and as much as it killed her, that meant leaving Mackenzie behind too. "Sorry, Mack, but you don't have a choice."

His eyes glowed with emotion. "Claire—"

"No, Mack. I'm not yours. I never have been."

Chapter Thirteen

Claire sipped on her mojito and stared out over Chandon Island's pristine white beach and the turquoise ocean gently lapping against the shoreline. If that wasn't spectacular enough, in an hour or so there'd be another breathtaking sunset. Beauty all around her, and yet it didn't really touch her inside.

She was living a dream life, but everything felt so damn empty.

At least she didn't have to worry about her sisters now. She hadn't wanted someone else to tell them she was a call girl, so she'd finally told them the truth. Tina and Danni had been shocked at first, and then outraged, before guilt had set in.

Acceptance had only come after she'd told them she no longer needed to work in the sex industry. Not with the sale of the house exceeding even the most hopeful outcome.

The money would set Tina and Danni up for years to come. They could now focus on their studies and hopefully not too much on what their older sister had done to pay the bills. And if study didn't distract them, she had no doubt all the men they effortlessly attracted would.

Not that they were alone in that regard.

She smiled politely at the good-looking man with tattooed sleeves a few stools down the beach-hut bar. He'd been trying to catch her eye half the afternoon. She sighed. Maybe she should have covered her white bikini with more than the colorful sarong she'd wrapped around her waist. Except she was so used to wearing little to nothing it'd been second nature to slip into yet another flimsy swimsuit.

Besides, there was no point in dressing in anything else when she did little more than swim in the freshwater pool, or snorkel in the ocean to admire the gorgeous reef and fish. And it wasn't as if any of the tropical island's five restaurants with their first-class menus interested her. Unlike the plentiful beverages she'd been busy sampling.

A pretty brunette arrived and sat on the barstool next to the tattooed man. He turned a subdued inked shoulder Claire's way to focus on the other woman. Claire sighed again. Did all men want what they couldn't have? Was the one woman in their grasp always the one they wanted the least?

Or maybe she really was jaded, thanks to the profession she'd left behind a little over three weeks ago. She took another mouthful of her refreshing but rather strong mojito. She mightn't be so insightful about other people's relationships if only her thoughts didn't constantly stray to what she'd had with Mackenzie.

He'd said he loved her and she'd discarded his words as though they'd meant nothing. But it was those same words that scared her more than anything else in the world. If he'd hurt her in the past, then imagining a future with a man she trusted, a man she lived and breathed for, gave her chills.

She didn't even want to think about the pain she'd endure when he finally walked away. She wouldn't—couldn't—put herself out there like that.

"Can I get you anything else, ma'am?" the bartender asked.

She glanced down at her empty drink. *Shit.* She'd guzzled it down fast. She nodded at the bartender, yet another man who'd been making unsubtle eyes at her. But with his blond, surfer good looks, she imagined he was a born flirt. "I might try another of your whiskey sours."

She'd sampled more than a couple of them these last few weeks.

He grinned, as though charmed by her praise of his bar skills. "Coming right up."

She downed another two before she thanked him and headed to the nearby pool on surprisingly wobbly legs. She really should eat solid food instead of the liquid lunch and dinners she'd been tossing back.

She hiccuped and giggled, before unknotting her sarong and sliding into the blissfully cool water. Ignoring a whistle of appreciation from a knot of young men at another open bar close to the pool, she forced her suddenly uncoordinated limbs to pull her through the water.

Twenty minutes later, her muscles aching and her breath rasping, she dragged herself out of the water. She should be tired and ready to sleep off her overindulgence of alcohol. Instead she was restless and self-aware, her nipples beading and her belly clenching.

She slung the sarong over a shoulder and headed back to the beach-hut bar. If she had to slurp back a dozen more drinks to forget about Mackenzie, she'd do precisely that. This new start was meant to help her forget about him, not keep her in a highly aroused state of yearning.

"Back again," the barman said with a pleased smile. "What's your fancy this round?"

She waved a careless hand. "Surprise me."

"Now that I can do."

He poured her some kind of creamy cocktail, and her taste buds danced in shock at the potent mix. She swallowed with a gasp. "Are you *trying* to make me drunk?"

He shrugged. "It looks to me like you're aiming to forget a certain someone. I'm in the business of doing exactly that."

She stifled a giggle. Oh, if only this young man knew the real her. The woman who'd probably had more sex than he'd poured drinks. The woman who'd heard every come-on line and then some. She sighed. He wouldn't understand. Not like Mackenzie.

Mack hadn't just been the only man to make her feel special, he'd been the only one who knew her better than anyone else. The only man who'd put her above his own needs, both physically and mentally.

"Hey, are you okay?"

The barman's voice jerked her out of her melancholic mood and back to the present. "Sorry, I'm fine, really." She managed a semblance of a smile, the late afternoon air now chilling her skin. The nights had been pleasantly cool compared to the hot days, and a bikini was no longer adequate for the drop in temperature. "Clearly I've had too much to drink." She stood, even as her surroundings did a slow twirl. "Time to sleep it off."

The barman frowned. "You don't look too good. My shift ends in a few minutes. Let me make sure you get home in one piece."

She was in no state to argue, and in fact was grateful for his strong forearm as she stumbled in the direction of her ground-floor apartment. She turned to him at the door. "Thanks for bringing me home. You're a great escort." She giggled, shook her head and repeated "*Escort*. You have no idea how funny that is!"

He cocked a blond brow, the insinuation going right over his head. "I'm just glad to see you happy."

She blinked hazily up at him. Damn, he was almost as tall as Mackenzie. A pity that's where any similarity ended. Mackenzie wasn't just a suited god with a charisma to match, he knew exactly what to say at the right time; knew precisely how to please her. She managed a smile. "Have I been that much of a sour-puss?"

"No." He stared at her, as though transfixed. "You've just looked incredibly sad." He leaned toward her, and she stood her ground even as she mentally backed away. She'd hoped this once a man had simply wanted to help her out, without expecting anything in return. She'd been wrong.

"Don't do this, Claire."

The barman jerked back before she had a chance to reject his advances. Goose bumps peppered her arms and need pooled deep in her womb as she slowly turned to face the one man she truly *did* want.

She swallowed hard. Mackenzie looked fiercely handsome in his dark jeans and leather jacket. But even with her eyes not quite focused and her mind not functioning at its best, she was conscious that his face was drawn, with dark shadows under his brilliant stare.

Somehow she wasn't surprised to see him here, not when she'd been so restless and aware all day. Perhaps she would have sensed him if not for her excessive drinking.

Mackenzie's stare glittered as he stared at her and then glanced at the barman. His mouth thinned when he turned back to her. "Or should I call you Scarlet again now?"

She swayed, feeling fragile and fighting back sudden tears. "I thought you were better than that," she whispered. God, this man really did have the power to hurt her. She managed to lift her chin. "What does it matter anyway? We're not together. You're not even my client anymore."

The dawning comprehension on the barman's face might have been funny under any other circumstances. Except now he'd judge her in a whole new light. She squeezed her eyes shut for a second, fighting for composure.

The barman was the least of her concerns.

Mackenzie's eyes darkened even as they glowed, much like the twilight beginning to settle around them. "If you care anything at all for me, you won't go inside with that man tonight."

She frowned, making sense of his words even though her mind was muddled. "Is that really what you thought was going to happen?"

But of course it was. She'd been a call girl. Did she really expect him to believe better of her now even though she'd left that industry?

The barman put out his hands. "Look, I don't know what is going on with you two and it's probably none of my business." He turned to Mackenzie. "But I'm guessing you're the reason this gorgeous lady's been so sad." He shook his head. "Looks like you've got a lot of making up to do."

Claire blinked. She hadn't expected that. Just like she hadn't expected Mackenzie's devotion. Except he'd always been her biggest supporter, and though he'd wanted her all to himself, he'd never cheapened her or made her feel less of a person.

She exhaled in a rush, her belly tightening with nausea. How had she messed things up so badly?

~

The roaring in Mackenzie's ears settled into a low-level drone as the barman walked away. He'd been prepared to fight for Claire, but he'd stayed cool and in control. In fact, most of his anger had been directed at himself.

He'd been a damn fool. Not just for allowing her to walk away from him the first time, but for then being the one who'd walked out on her.

He'd had long talks with her sisters, and uncovered much of Claire's past and many of her issues. He'd needed all the ammunition and knowledge he could glean in order to win her back.

Not only had she lost her mother and raised her sisters, she'd faced abandonment by her own father. She'd grown up believing men were faithless and dishonorable. And she'd managed those beliefs by getting paid by those same faithless men, taking care of her sisters and debts at the same time.

Not that Claire's career had exactly been a win–win. She'd been treading a fine line, a balancing act that left no room for error. His being with Claire had destabilized her, shaken her convictions. Little wonder she'd run the first time. His leaving her the second time had probably convinced her she'd been right about men all along.

But he was here now to prove, once and for all, that her theories of him and men in general were skewed. Everyone had faults and no-one was perfect. Yes, there were bad and selfish men—and women—in the world. But there were also many more good men with generous hearts who wanted nothing more than to find their soulmate. To make that woman their wife, and to have kids, a family.

Men like him.

Claire groaned, clutched at her belly and swayed. He strode forward, tucking one arm around her waist to keep her balanced, his other hand smoothing back the strands of hair that'd been loosened by her swim.

When she subsided against him, he asked gently, "Are you okay?"

She shook her head, her profile porcelain pale. "Not really."

He guided her inside. Closing the front door behind them, he headed down a short hallway to where he guessed the bathroom was located. A shower would sober her up. She didn't say a word as he unclipped her bikini top and pulled down its bottom.

He swallowed, doing all he could not to react to her nakedness, if only his body listened. He wasn't in the habit of getting a hard-on for someone drunk, even if that someone was the same beautiful woman he was in love with.

He turned on the taps a little more forcefully than necessary before Claire stepped under the heat. She swayed, and when her legs buckled, he reached into the stall to keep her balanced, before he stepped inside with her, fully dressed.

Holding her steady with one hand, he unclipped her hair and reached for the shampoo. Her breasts mashed against his drenched shirt and jacket. He gritted his teeth and ignored the rush of blood to his dick.

Bloody hell. It was going to be a long night.

Everything he wanted to tell her would now have to wait until the morning.

Chapter Fourteen

Claire woke with her body cramping with rebellion and her memory fuzzy around the edges. She inhaled deep, a thrill riding through her. Even without Mackenzie's dark-spiced cologne on her pillow, she remembered enough to know he was here.

He'd held her in his arms last night, no expectations, no whispered promises, nothing but the emotional support she'd craved. And going by the indent on the mattress, he hadn't long been out of bed.

She sat at hearing his familiar tread, the scent of coffee and toast pervading her nostrils as she stared blearily at him. Damn. At this time of morning no-one had the right to look *that* healthy and fresh, not to mention sexy as hell.

He placed a tray beside her, his eyes warm. "Toast with vegemite, and coffee, black and strong."

She fought back sudden nausea even as her belly grumbled. "You really are my knight in shining armor." Her eyes widened as she finally noticed his clothes ... or lack of them. Not that he didn't wear his boxer briefs and black T-shirt perfectly well.

He smirked. "My clothes got a little wet last night when it looked like you might pass out in the shower." He shrugged. "My jeans are still in the dryer and my leather jacket ... I don't know that it'll ever recover. Guess I should be grateful I decided to wear something under my jeans for travelling."

She pressed a hand to her mouth, vague recollections returning to her of him holding her while hot water pummelled down. "God, you must think I'm the biggest idiot."

His grin faded, his eyes turning serious. "Confused. Frightened. Wary. Yes. An idiot—never." He passed her the toast. "Here, take a bite. It will make you feel better."

She nodded, then chewed and swallowed. "How did you know where to find me?"

"Your sisters were quite forthcoming." He sat on the edge of the bed. "I knew you needed a bit of time to yourself first. And I needed to sort out a hundred and one business commitments to have some time off. Once that was done I arranged a private charter from Sydney to Hamilton Island before taking a ferry here."

She sucked down some scalding coffee, needing the caffeine fix like nothing else. She looked up. "You really don't give up easily, do you?"

"Not for the woman I want. Not without a fight." He exhaled softly. "I almost lost you once, I was a fool to think I could let you go a second time."

Warmth pooled in her belly. For a shrewd and clever man he sure took his time accepting the truth. "You must know you're nothing like your father."

He nodded. "Yes. I just ... lost it when I saw Bradley forcing himself on you." His hands fisted at the memory. "I wanted to kill him."

Her heart melted for him. "You're human, and you wanted to protect me. I'm grateful you feel that way about me."

His eyes darkened. "I feel that way and a whole lot more."

She swallowed. "Even though I've slept with other men for money?"

"Claire, I've paid you and other women for sex. Do you really think I care about any of that?" He shook his head. "I only care about you ... about us." His voice lowered. "About our future."

Warmth swept through her body, but she ignored the rising elation for just a little longer, and placed her mug of coffee onto the bedside table. "Why me? I mean, you could have any woman you wanted."

"And you could have any man you wanted," he said huskily. He blew out a breath. "I watched you most of the day yesterday, biding my time and waiting for the right moment to approach. I felt like a starved man watching prey."

She smiled at the imagery. "I think I sensed you."

He arched a dark brow. "I thought you might have been too busy deflecting men everywhere you went." He leaned forward, his hand clasping her chin, his thumb rubbing back and forth. "You're an incredibly beautiful woman, Claire. I can't blame men for wanting what I want so damn badly too."

"And when I get older and my beauty fades?" she whispered. "What then?"

Would he abandon her like her father had abandoned her mother?

"You'll still be beautiful in my eyes." He bent and kissed her gently, then murmured, "We'll grow old together, with thousands of photos showing off our youth."

She reached out to put her toast next to her abandoned coffee mug. "Are you saying you *want* to grow old with me?"

He nodded, lying next to her on the bed and cupping the back of her head with one hand, his other moving up to trace her lips as he murmured huskily, "I want that more than anything else."

She blinked up at him, her eyes wide and heart thudding with thrilling hope. His entire body sang with honesty, his warm embrace telling her she had nothing more to fear. Nothing more to run from. He wasn't going anywhere. It was all up to her now.

He waited patiently, before she nodded and said, "I want that too."

His eyes lit up even as they darkened with desire, with joy. Then he was kissing her, his big body moving to cover hers. Her lashes fluttered and her womb heated. God, it'd been too long since she'd made love. Mackenzie's mouth stayed on hers as he peeled the bedcover and sheet back, allowing her to hook her ankles behind his waist.

He swallowed her quiet exhalation. She was desperate to feel his slick heat against her skin, impatient to have the hard length of his cock between her thighs.

He tore away only long enough to tug off his shirt and his boxer briefs. His back muscles rippled with the motion, his bared buttocks flexing. Then his mouth was all over hers again, his cock thick and strong against her belly, his chest rubbing against her soft breasts and hardening nipples.

Heat rippled through her body, moisture dewing between her thighs. She needed him so badly. Every cell was attuned to him, her nerve endings dancing with desire. Even her breaths in and out were heated. Like she existed just for these moments with Mackenzie.

He pushed a finger into her, ensuring she was wet for him. She closed her eyes on a shuddering breath, squirming beneath him. Need, want, yearning, desire ... it was all she could think about.

Her eyes popped open when he centered his cock between the petals of her sex and didn't move any further. "Mack ... don't stop now," she groaned.

But, though passion radiated off him in waves, determination was just as powerful. "Do you want me in your bed for the rest of your life?" he half-growled, a vein throbbing in his brow at the restraint.

She dug her nails into his forearms. He chose *now* to make her answer such a serious question? But of course he did. She wouldn't hold back on an answer when she was ten seconds away from glorious fulfilment. "Yes, Mack. Yes, I do."

Something glinted behind his stare. Satisfaction. Relief. Joy. And then his hips drove forward and his cock filled her to the limit, and all she could think about was their joining. Not just physically. It was as if their hearts and their souls had joined too.

She whimpered, overwhelmed with emotion.

Sex with other men had been nothing more than a physical connection. Every sexual encounter with Mackenzie had gone beyond simple intimacy. But it'd never been this powerful, this hyper-aware and exhilarating.

He paused. "You feel it too?" he asked hoarsely.

She swallowed, and nodded. "Yes."

He kissed her then, their joining even more emphatic. She didn't fight it, didn't want to rebel against this absolute rightness, this feeling of being whole for once in her life.

He released her mouth only as he took up an ever-increasing rhythm that she counter-matched stroke for stroke. His burning eyes held hers as she inhaled sharply, balancing on the precipice. She fell apart in a rush of exhalation, toppling into nirvana and into the arms of a fierce climax.

He closed his eyes and threw his head back, groaning as he climaxed, his seed shooting long and deep.

He didn't draw away from her, instead he kept his weight on his forearms and stayed connected and watched her slowly come back to earth. "Tell me you meant every word," he said hoarsely.

She blinked up at him, her whole body drowsy and sated, with not even an inkling of sickness churning her belly. "I meant every word." She smiled up at him. "Mack, is this your way of proposing?"

He smiled back, his eyes gleaming with emotion. "It wasn't exactly the way I'd meant to do it—the ring I had designed is in the pocket in my jacket—but *yes*, it is my way of proposing." His thumb traced over her lips, his voice serious as he asked, "Claire, will you marry me, and make me the happiest man alive?"

Her smile turned into a face-stretching grin. "Yes, Mack. I'd like nothing more than to make you the happiest man alive by marrying you."

He kissed her with a tenderness that touched her deeply, before he said huskily, "I love you, Claire."

She blinked, her heart swelling with emotion. "And I love you, Mackenzie Smitherson." She bit her bottom lip. "Just one thing."

He pulled his head back. "Yes?"

"How much did you pay Maisey to be with me for the weekend?"

He chuckled. "I paid twice what your clients would have paid." He smirked. "She severely underestimated how far I was prepared to go to make you mine."

Claire blew a piece of hair from her brow. "Maisey made more than enough money from me."

He nodded, his stare a little more somber. "And what about you?"

"What about me?"

"Your sisters told me you gave them all the money from the sale of the house."

She shrugged. "I've saved enough to keep me going for quite some time."

He kissed her on the nose and gently pulled free. "You won't ever need to worry about finances again."

She blinked. He was beyond wealthy, that much was obvious. But being a pampered wife had never been a part of her plans. She rubbed the back of her neck. Perhaps she could volunteer at a women's shelter, or fund an organization to help abandoned women come to terms with their loss. "I don't know how I feel about that."

He rolled onto his side and reached for her toast, before proffering it to her. She took another bite even as he said, "Why wouldn't you be happy? The only man you ever need to keep content will be me ... your future husband."

She pushed the toast back toward him. When he took the next cold bite, she said huskily, "Well then, I guess I'd better get in some more practice." She climbed on top, straddling him with a silken smile as his appreciative gaze drank in her nudity.

"Practice does make perfect," he agreed, crust dangling from his hand.

She smirked, happiness filling her from the inside out. "Then you really are going to be the happiest husband alive."

Epilogue

Claire straightened the 'selfie' Mack had taken of them on the cliff face what seemed like a lifetime ago. She smiled at the memory. They'd made so many more memories since that day a little over two months ago.

She touched their wedding portrait taken just a week ago. It'd been a small and intimate ceremony with just their sisters, his secretary Matilda, along with her husband, and his two young execs, Terry and Regan as witnesses.

Her hand moved to the next framed photo displaying Danni and Tina at her wedding with the two handsome execs. The four had previously met at the surprise twenty-fifth birthday party Mackenzie had thrown Claire, where he'd then handed her back the keys to the house she'd grown up in.

She smiled, her eyes then drawn to the group photo where all her family and friends—including her call girl friends—screamed out 'cheese' for the photo, balancing their party hats on their heads with one hand and holding birthday cake with the other.

Tears welled. She was so lucky to be surrounded by so many people she loved and who loved her in return. Not that anyone could possibly shower her with as much affection as her husband.

She should have known Mackenzie had been the buyer of the house she and her sisters had grown up in. Should have known because he'd bid far more than the house had been worth. But he'd given her the opportunity to set up a home for women needing refuge and temporary shelter, allowed her to put into practice her desire to help those who needed it most.

People like Emma.

She'd become good friends with her sister-in-law, and a good listener on those rare moments when Emma had needed to unburden some of the horror she'd faced in her past. Mackenzie's sister might still quietly grieve, but she was gaining strength away from the monster she'd married, and who'd almost killed her spirit.

Claire was convinced that helping to run the refuge had done more to heal Emma's inner wounds than any amount of therapy would have.

Her stare returned to the photo of her gorgeous sisters and their new boyfriends. Who'd have thought they would have gotten along so famously? In fact, things had become pretty serious between them in record time. It'd made her realize her 'little' sisters weren't so little anymore.

She splayed a hand over her belly. It was probably a good thing. Her period was two weeks late and her hormones were already doing crazy things to her emotions. She chewed on her bottom lip. It looked like this year things were going to take an even bigger leap into a bright and dazzling future. Mackenzie stepped behind her, his breath warm on her scalp and his hands curling over her shoulders in a possessive touch. "Terry and Regan are good men. You have nothing to worry about."

Claire smiled and nodded, before refocusing on the picture. "I know. I need to let my sisters lead their own lives now." She turned in his arms, smiling as his stare strayed over the parts of her exposed in her plunging rainbow gown. "So ... any plans for today?"

"Since our honeymoon is almost over, I thought we might take one last leisurely picnic at the falls."

She kept her smirk all on the inside. Visiting the Blue Mountain's art galleries and tourist shops had obviously worn thin. Cocking her head to the side, she teased, "No need to pack our swimsuits then?"

He bent and kissed her, telling her without words how much he loved her. When he finally drew back, he said huskily, "No need at all."

She blinked back more happy tears. She'd wait until they were at the beautiful falls to tell him the news. Her heart all but sang. If she'd thought life couldn't get any better, she'd been wrong. Happiness was no longer a pipe dream. It was hers to live every waking moment.

The End

Want more VIP Desire Agency stories by Mel Teshco...

Exclusive

Also included in the VIP Desire Agency Boxset

A rock star and an escort. What could possibly go wrong?

Amos Drynn isn't interested in a relationship. He's been there, done that, and wished he'd listened to his better judgment. As the lead singer of the famous band Frankenstein's Blood, he's not short of female attention, but in his world, a long term relationship isn't feasible. That is, until he purchases a night with a call girl who makes his blood run hot and has him forgetting all about his fear of commitment.

Tiffany doesn't believe in fairytales, not anymore. In her world trust is thin on the ground and promises are meaningless, especially from the mouth of a married client. A night in bed with her rock idol, Amos Drynn, will surely salve her wounded pride. But will their explosive chemistry shatter her infatuation with an ex-client or will she turn her back on Amos, the one man willing to give her everything, including his heart?

Chapter One of Exclusive

The raspy, soulful voice of Amos Drynn, the lead singer of Frankenstein's Blood, swept over Tiffany like a dark caress. But she ignored the prickling of awareness that rippled over her skin and instead showed the backdoor bouncers her VIP pass.

She smiled at security as they stepped aside to allow her past and into the converted warehouse. Chin tilted high, she ignored their lustful stares as the heels of her sharp-tipped stilettos clicked down the corridor as though she'd taken to the catwalk.

She'd acted the part of temptress and femme fatale enough times to slip into its comfortable skin, and to expect both men and women to involuntarily stare. Her smile widened. To expect men, and occasionally women, to want her badly enough to pay for the privilege.

Not that it was just about looks. She'd learned early in her profession that charisma was as much about confidence and poise, and taking genuine interest in a client. She'd also learned that sometimes the wealthiest and best looking men weren't getting their deepest needs met, sexually, or emotionally.

Despite the soundproof walls, the powerful music grew in volume as Amos belted out one more song she knew word-for-word.

I want a faithful lover
A woman I can trust
Don't need a second mother
Our passion turning to dust
It's you and me, baby
You're my one and only...

Her gut pulled with envy at the woman who'd one day be just that for Amos and more. Unlike Tiffany, whose very profession ensured such a feat was near impossible.

A sudden flurry of nerves struck deep in her belly, leaving her nauseous. There were times, like now, when her confidence suddenly deserted her, when anxiety sucked away all positive emotion. Her hand shook as she opened her black clutch and slipped her VIP pass inside. The ticket would be a keepsake she'd treasure forever.

Drawing in a deep, steadying breath, she slowed as she neared the stage doors where a couple of roadies in their standard dusty jeans and logoed t-shirts watched the wrap-up of the show from the sidelines.

They didn't glance her way. They were probably well used to women hovering around the fringes, whether it was girlfriends, lovers, or wives. Not to mention paid women like herself.

After her friend and fellow call girl, Scarlet, had left behind her professional life and moved onto a brighter than bright future, Tiffany had jumped at the job offer that had come her way. Her mouth dried. What woman wouldn't want to become Amos' latest companion? But unlike Scarlet and her other friend Brandy, not every call girl was lucky enough to have a client fall in love with them.

After a failed affair with a client who was also a married man, Tiffany knew better than most that the men she met in her line of work weren't always honorable. She sighed. If Toby hadn't been her client, she mightn't now be so cynical about every other man's intentions. Instead, she'd discovered that falling in love was a huge mistake, one she didn't ever care to repeat.

She drew in another steadying breath. She'd make the most out of this assignment, her feelings firmly disconnected, just the way her client expected.

The lead singer of Frankenstein's Blood wouldn't be impressed if he knew she was a huge fan. So she'd pretend disinterest. It was why she'd deliberately avoided the concert until it was almost over. Now that she was doing her best to put Toby behind her, she'd resume her professional role, and stay that way until she was out of the call girl business for good.

That won't be happening anytime soon. She squeezed her eyes shut, doing her best to ignore the snide voice, and once again push aside the constant gnawing ache that pressed in on her from all sides.

A little over five years ago, her father had been crushed by a truck while he'd been unloading from it with a forklift. His head and spinal injuries meant he'd needed a specially designed house and full-time care. Sending him to a nursing home wasn't even an option; it'd send her once independent dad to an early grave.

How different both their lives might be right now if her mother hadn't run off with her dad's best friend... if her mother hadn't left behind Tiffany as a twelve-year-old to be raised by the man who'd been left crushed in spirit long before the truck had done the same to his body.

Tiffany's lashes fluttered apart. She didn't need her mom. She'd gotten out of the financial mess by working as an escort, and would continue to work as one for a long as it paid the bills and she'd saved enough for a secure future.

In the meantime, if Amos wanted the public to see a sexy and beautiful woman on his arm, one without any baggage, then that was what she'd give him. She wouldn't be throwing herself at him, or fall to pieces like some rabid teenage girl. She'd repress all of her fangirl enthusiasm.

It shouldn't be too hard a feat, not after Toby had blackened her heart with empty promises and meaningless assurances.

Sensing the attention of the roadies, she forced a smile their way. Their stares slid back to the stage as Amos' husky tone soared into a controlled tenor, and then cut off with the conclusion of the song.

The crowd roared, clapping thunderously even as Amos thanked the Sydney crowd for their support and said goodnight.

She swallowed hard. In a matter of seconds, she'd finally meet the lead singer of Frankenstein's Blood, whose raw ballads never failed to twist her insides with yearning, and whose powerful lyrics could rocket her from misery to a rush of powerful, positive emotions.

She'd soon find out all there was to know about her rock star idol. But the cynical part of her wondered if disappointment would override any and all starstruck emotion once she got to know the real him.

Life wasn't fairytales and rainbows, no matter how much she worked at making her clients believe just that.

The lead guitarist, Jaimee Redden—J.R. to all his fans—walked through the opened stage doors. His eyes widened at seeing her, before he winked and drawled, "Hey, baby, looking for me?"

Even if she hadn't sensed his swaggering self-importance, she would have smelled the whiskey on his breath a mile away.

She resisted stepping back. "No, I'm here for Amos."

Jaimee shook his head, his long, curly hair bouncing, and his eyes hardening as he looked her over again with a curled lip. "Like he needs to pay a woman to fuck and have a good time."

She'd met people like Jaimee. Deep down, they were insecure nobodies who tried to make her feel less high-class and more cheap whore. All of them were hypocrites at best and this man was no different. It was more than obvious he took advantage of the groupies. She could well imagine his personal motto. *Why pay for the cow when I can get the milk for free?*

At least she didn't exploit her clients. Men like Amos were more than willing to exchange cash for pleasure.

She smiled sweetly. "I guess you get what you pay for."

A dark, sexy chuckle sent little shivers down her spine, and she turned as Amos stepped toward her and murmured, "Not to mention less trouble, more fun."

The lead guitarist faded from existence as she swallowed past her suddenly dry throat. Up close and personal, Amos was pure masculine sin. Tall and broad, his powerful arms could easily hold a woman up against a wall while he fucked her into submission. His skin was damp with sweat, and she stifled an urge to inhale his musky scent deep into her lungs, then lick his tattooed arms and follow wherever the ink led.

Amos paused, his tight leather pants outlining an impressive bulge. Her womb clenched. Sex with most of her clients was just part of her job description, mostly pleasurable and occasionally boring. But nothing about Amos would be dull. Everything about him was exciting and she craved to get him naked and even more gloriously sweaty.

He cocked his head to the side, his stare gleaming with approval. "You must be Tiffany."

She managed a nod and a smile, her pulse beating out of rhythm and her skills as a conversationalist scattered like dust to the wind. Amos made her feel as skittish as a newly handled filly, yet sexy in a whole new way, like she was a virgin stepping out in the form-fitting, little black dress for the very first time.

"You're happy to go to the afterparty with me, yes?" he asked, looking amused by her tongue-tied silence.

She nodded again, and then managed, "Yes, of course. I'm looking forward to it."

Hopefully it wouldn't be too out there. She'd heard what went on at some afterparties. But she couldn't back out now. Her reputation was at stake, along with the VIP Desire Agency she worked for. Besides, those afterparties were one of the reasons he paid for an escort. He wanted to keep the crazies at bay, at the same time he fostered his wild boy image.

The rest of the band members marched past, a bearded man wolf-whistling in appreciation as he all but undressed Tiffany with his eyes.

Amos cocked a brow. "Piss off, Tommy, she's mine."

She recognized Tommy, he was the talented drummer whose beats held together the rock ballads, and became the frenzied, driving pulse of the heavier rock tunes. He scraped a hand over his closely shorn hair and grinned carelessly. "You always get the cream of the crop, lucky bastard."

Amos returned the grin. "Only lucky in that I have impeccable taste."

Tommy shook his head ruefully and disappeared into a door further down the corridor, the same room the rest of the band members had entered.

Amos swept out a hand. "After you, gorgeous Tiffany. I need to shower and change at my hotel before we leave for the afterparty."

She looked up at him as they strolled down the corridor, grateful he slowed his long-legged stride to accommodate her smaller steps. "I could have met you at your hotel room?"

"Yes. But I thought you might enjoy the concert first."

She hid a wry smile. "I'm not really a fan." The lie came all too easily after she'd put her trust in Toby. Her former client and lover had damaged a part of her that she had doubts would ever heal. She'd never expose the vulnerable part of her heart ever again. Not for any man.

Amos' breath whistled through his lips. "Ouch. Shot down in flames!"

Despite her best intentions, she giggled at his mock outrage, sounding more like a silly schoolgirl than the classy woman he'd no doubt envisaged. It didn't stop him from smiling and curling an arm around her, his big, sweaty body pressed against her slender frame, and his large hand covering much of her bared skin through the backless dress.

Somehow, she didn't mind, not even a little. His touch burned through her flesh and awakened dormant nerve endings, her knees going weak. What woman wouldn't have melted into a puddle of bliss at his touch? What woman wouldn't die just a little to be underneath his warm, honed body?

The opened door revealed a VIP lounge, where at least a dozen women vied for the band members' attention. One young woman in a minidress and chunky-heeled boots had already locked lips with Jaimee, both of them seemingly oblivious to their audience.

Tiffany resisted rolling her eyes. J.R. was a jerk, plain and simple. She only wished the groupie with stars in her eyes knew better. But Tiffany was grateful at least that none of the other women saw Amos bypass the room. She wanted him all to herself and was glad she didn't have to watch him fend off a dozen screaming fans, before their hostile eyes turned her way.

Despite the fact her profession paid the bills and saved her father from rotting in an old people's home, it wasn't an easy career. Little wonder her anxieties had been triggered tonight.

She exhaled once they were safely out of range of the VIP lounge. Her next inhalation dragged in Amos' delicious, musky sweat mixed with something exotic and dark. She resisted sighing. He probably had cologne made especially for him.

When something close to a purr instead rumbled deep in her throat, she gulped down the sound and distracted herself by taking in the converted warehouse building. Even with limited theater seating and tickets at a premium price, she'd heard it was the offstage shadowy intimacy, contrasting ocher walls and eclectic prints, reminiscent of bold art deco, that helped secure many top performers.

Not that Frankenstein's Blood needed the incentive of money. They'd be rolling in it already.

The bouncers she'd seen earlier barely hid their knowing smirks as they opened the back exit doors to allow her and Amos outside. Amos then led her through the reserved parking lot, to a shiny red muscle car that screamed V8 power.

He opened her passenger door, a true gentleman, and she smiled up at him and said, "Nice car."

He grinned. "Meet Suzy, my '69 Ford Mustang." His sigh sounded almost forlorn. "They don't make cars like they used to."

The door clunked shut behind her before he folded his big body into the driver's seat and turned the ignition. The engine roared into life before he backed the car out with practiced ease.

Once out on the street, he glanced at her, the flash of streetlights revealing the interested glint of his eyes. "So tell me about yourself."

Clients never asked about her private life, and she wasn't about to be an open book to the first client who showed interest. She smothered a sigh. It was bad enough Toby had learned so much about her. She shrugged and said in an offhand tone, "What can I say? I'm a call girl. I fuck rich men like you for money."

His teeth gleamed in the gloom. "What can I say? I like your honesty."

"No point in pretending I'm something I'm not."

"True." His hands curled easily around the steering wheel, his energy after his big performance clearly not diminished. "I imagine taking care of a man's physical needs is both a risky and rewarding profession."

She looked his way, trying not to lower her defenses. He might be a rock god, but she sensed he was also a genuinely nice guy. Then again, she'd been wrong before. "Yes."

He indicated to turn at the T-intersection ahead. "You don't like talking about yourself. Is that a call girl thing?"

She ignored the peculiar burning sensation in her chest when she asked, "I don't know. Did Scarlet?"

He exhaled and then cleared his throat. "To be honest, I wouldn't know. I never asked her anything personal." He glanced her way. "Not once."

She refused to allow his revelation to go to her head.

Instead, she conceded, "Call girls don't encourage personal topics. We tend to listen, not chat about ourselves." She looked his way. "It's all part of our service."

He nodded. "I get it."

She smiled, changing the subject and adding huskily, "So let's talk about you."

A faint frown wrinkled his brow. "You know, you don't need to act the call girl, not for me. I'm happy for you to be yourself."

She blinked. If he only knew how much she really did want to know about him. "I'm genuinely interested to hear more about you, especially the person behind the singer."

He shrugged, evidently going along with her interest. "On stage, I'm basically public property. Offstage, I'm an intensely private person, despite the spotlight. Give me country peace and quiet to the frenetic pace of the city any day."

He stopped at a red traffic light, for a moment his attention turning wholly to her. "Other than that, there's not all that much to tell. I sing and hope someone will be inspired in some way... or at the very least enjoy my music."

She knew without a doubt he had a whole lot more to share, but she wasn't in the business to push for information. He'd tell her what he wanted, and she was happy with that. After all, he wasn't the only one keeping things private. She lived in a whole different world to the life she had as a call girl.

Still, she couldn't help but add, "Your music influences thousands of fans. I imagine it's a heady feeling."

He nodded. "It is. But it's also daunting at times. What if I write a song that negatively affects someone?" He glanced back at her. "What if I sing something that reminds someone of an incident they'd rather forget?"

She couldn't help but smile. "Sometimes being reminded about something you'd rather forget is a good thing. No matter how negative it might feel at the time."

"It sounds as though you're speaking from experience."

She'd already told him she wasn't a fan. There was no way she was going to admit to the devastation she'd experienced on hearing the one song that'd reminded her all too vividly of Toby's betrayal. A reminder she needed to have so as to never let something like it happen again.

Instead, she shrugged and said, "Maybe."

He rubbed at his brow, his voice dry. "I'll have to remember you don't talk about yourself. So let's talk about something else?"

Her taut shoulders relaxed. "Sure."

He glanced her way, his stare glinting. "I imagine affecting people so effortlessly with your looks and charisma must also be a heady feeling?"

She hid a smile. As a handsome as hell rock god, he'd understand all too well.

But she'd play along. "It can be daunting at times too. High expectations and all that."

He chuckled. "Well, you have nothing to fear from me. I have no expectations aside from enjoying looking at you while we socialize until some ungodly hour of the morning."

The car dashboard was already inching toward midnight. The hours would tick by far too quickly for her liking. Still, she couldn't help but wonder if maybe he didn't find her attractive enough to take to bed. Or maybe he wasn't attracted to the opposite sex, period. No. There was too much sexual tension between them to imagine he wasn't interested.

When Amos pulled up at a hotel that gleamed golden under its many lights, and which washed him in a glow that made him appear even more magnificent, she shivered with yearning.

Even Toby hadn't affected her with this carnal need that had her pulse hammering and her womb clenching. No client or lover had made her feel this intensity of need.

A valet appeared out of seemingly nowhere and opened Tiffany's door. She smiled thanks before the young man handed Amos a claim ticket in exchange for a large tip. The valet beamed approval and jumped into the car to drive it to the parking area beneath the hotel.

Amos stepped toward her and held out his arm. “Let the night begin.”

If you would like to know when my next book is available, news, cover reveals and more, you can sign up for my newsletter: madmimi.com/signups/121695/join

Check out my website – http://www.melteshco.com/

You can also friend me on Facebook at https://www.facebook.com/mel.teshco

Or on my author Facebook page at https://www.facebook.com/MelTeshcoAuthor

And occasionally on Twitter at https://twitter.com/melteshco

Contact me: melteshco@yahoo.com.au

If you enjoy my books I'd be delighted if you would consider leaving a review. This will help other readers find my books.

About the Author

Mel Teshco loves to write scorching sci-fi and contemporary stories with an occasional paranormal thrown into the mix. Not easy with seven cats, two dogs and a fat black thoroughbred vying for attention, especially when Mel's also busily stuffing around on Facebook. With only one daughter now living at home to feed two minute noodles, she still shakes her head at how she managed to write with three daughters and three stepchildren living under the same roof. Not to mention Mr. Semi-Patient (the one and same husband hoping for early retirement...he's been waiting a few years now.) Clearly anything is possible, even in the real world.

The VIP Desire Agency: series order
Lady in Red (book 1)
High Class (book 2)
Exclusive (book 3)
Liberated (book 4)
Uninhibited (book 5)
The VIP Desire Agency Boxed Set (all 5 books in the series)
The Virgin Hunt Games volume 1
The Virgin Hunt Games volume 2
The Virgin Hunt Games volume 3
Coming soon
The Virgin Hunt Games volumes 4-6
Alien Hunger: series order
Galactic Burn (book 1)
Galactic Inferno (book 2)
Galactic Flame (book 3)
Coming soon
Galactic Blaze (book 4)
Nightmix: series order:
Lusting the Enemy (book 1)
Abducting the Princess (book 2)
Seducing the Huntress (book 3)
Dragons of Riddich: series order:
Kadin (free prequel - book 1)
Asher (book 2)
Baron (book 3)
Dahlia (book 4)
Wyatt (book 5)
Valor (book 6)
The Queen (book 7)
Winged & Dangerous: series order
Stone Cold Lover (book 1)

Ice Cold Lover (book 2)
Red Hot Lover (book 3)
Winged & Dangerous Box Set (all 3 books in the series)
Box sets with authors Christina Phillips & Cathleen Ross
Taken by the Sheikh
Taken by the Billionaire
Taken by the Desert Sheikh
Resisting the Firefighter
Dirty Sexy Space continuity with authors Shona Husk and Denise Rossetti:
Yours to Uncover (book 1)
Mine to Serve (book 6)
Ours to Share (book 8)
Standalone longer length titles: (50k-100k)
Mutant Unveiled
Shadow Hunter
Highest Bid
As I Am
Existence
Standalone novellas and short stories: (15k-35K)
Identity Shift
Moon Thrall
Blood Chance
Carnal Moon
Stripped
Clarissa
Camilla
Selena's Bodyguard (also part of the Christmas Assortment Box)
Anthologies:
Down and Dusty: The Complete Collection
The Christmas Assortment Box
Secret Confessions: Sydney Housewives

Coming soon from December 2021: (Pre-order)
The Sheikh's Runaway Bride
The Sheikh's Captive Lover

Don't miss out!

Visit the website below and you can sign up to receive emails whenever Mel Teshco publishes a new book. There's no charge and no obligation.

https://books2read.com/r/B-A-ZFLB-NXRRB

www.ingramcontent.com/pod-product-compliance
Ingram Content Group UK Ltd.
Pitfield, Milton Keynes, MK11 3LW, UK
UKHW041823200726
13854UKWH00002BA/518